Who's got Gertie? And how can we get her back!

LINDA BAILEY

KIDS CAN PRESS

Kids Can Press acknowledges the financial support of the Ontario Arts Council, the
Canada Council for the Arts and the Government of Canada, through the BPIDP, for
our publishing activity.

Published in Canada by
Kids Can Press Ltd.
29 Birch Avenue
Toronto, ON M4V 1E2

Published in the U.S. by
Kids Can Press Ltd.
2250 Military Road
Tonawanda, NY 14150

www.kidscanpress.com

Edited by Charis Wahl
Interior designed by Tom Dart/First Folio Resource Group, Inc.
Printed and bound in Canada

Lyrics to "Hound Dog," p. 23, copyright © by Jerry Leiber and Mike Stoller

Many thanks to Charis Wahl — editor extraordinaire and the best friend Stevie
Diamond ever had.

CM 94 0 9 8 7 6

Library and Archives Canada Cataloguing in Publication

Bailey, Linda, 1948–
        Who's got Gertie? And how can we get her back!

ISBN-13: 978-1-55074-217-6 ISBN-10: 1-55074-217-5

I.Title.

PS8553.A3644W5 1994   jC813'.54   C94-931230-4
PZ7.B35Wh 1994

Kids Can Press is a **CORUS**™ Entertainment company

For my parents,
Addie and Harry Bailey,
with love and appreciation

CHAPTER

I T ALL STARTED WITH SAPPY RABBITS. THAT'S THE
summer day camp that me and my friend,
Jesse, almost got stuck in last August. It wasn't
really called Sappy Rabbits, of course. The ad that
came in the mail called it Happy Rabbits Summer
Adventures.

Jesse groaned when he saw the pink paper.
"Sappy Rabbits *Stupid* Adventures is more like it!"

The name stuck.

The ad said Sappy Rabbits was for six- to
twelve-year-olds. Don't you believe it. Nobody
over six and a half would be caught dead in the
place. Do you want to know how many things
were wrong with it? Have you got half an hour to
listen?

First of all, the hand-holding. The Sappy Rabbits
people seemed to think Vancouver was full of
vicious racing-car drivers just looking for innocent
kids to run down. Why else would they have
such a stupid rule? Those poor guys have to *hold
hands* when they cross the street! I've seen them.
A whole big snaky line of Sappy Rabbits!

Second, the activities. They may say the camp is for ages six to twelve, but they don't *really* expect twelve-year-olds like me and Jesse to show up. I looked in the window and, man, I saw play dough!

Then there's the hats. All Sappy Rabbits have to wear the official Sappy Rabbits hat. It's a big white sun-hat with a wide brim and — are you ready? — pink elastic under the chin. Around the brim are pink rabbits. *Dancing* pink rabbits, all with one leg waving around in the air.

A rabbit cancan. Puh-leeeeese.

Jesse and I told our parents that Sappy Rabbits was the dumbest idea they'd ever had. We reminded them we were almost teenagers. Not only that — we were experienced detectives who had solved two real, honest-to-goodness, dangerous crimes. Diamond & Kulniki Detective Agency, that's us. I'm the Diamond part — Stevie Diamond, short for Stephanie. Jesse is the Kulniki part. We had business cards and everything.

"That's just the point!" said my mom. "There's no telling what kind of trouble you two might get into if we leave you on your own. Besides, it will only be for a few weeks — just till school starts."

She and my dad, and Jesse's mom, too, were all busy working in August. They'd "feel better," she said, if they knew we were safe.

Right. *They'd* feel better. *We'd* be wearing dancing-rabbit hats.

Then, right at the last minute — just when it looked like there was no hope at all — Gertie Wiggins rescued us.

"I'd be glad to keep an eye on Stevie and Jesse," she told my mom.

Gertie Wiggins is this old actress who lives in the same housing co-op as me and Jesse. She's a bit weird, with her orange hair and all that bright make-up. But she's really nice to me and Jesse. And let's face it, if it meant getting out of Sappy Rabbits, I'd have let a werewolf look after me.

Anyway, that's how me and Jesse ended up hanging out with Gertie last August. And that's how we ended up helping her with her acting. And that's why, when she disappeared, we just *had* to get her back. It was a matter of life and ... Sappy Rabbits!

But maybe I better start with the morning of the last day we saw her. It was one of the hottest days of the year, and the three of us were in Gertie's apartment ...

CHAPTER

2

"**H**UM LOUDER!" I TOLD JESSE. "AND FLAP YOUR wings. Can't we *please* make this just a little more realistic?"

Jesse was crouched on a kitchen chair, his skinny arms sticking out straight. He gave me a dirty look.

"How come I always have to be the mosquito?"

"Mosqui*toes*," I said. "You're a swarm of giant, angry, hungry mosquitoes. Right, Gertie?"

Gertie squinted at her script. "Five mosquitoes," she said. "But they *are* pretty big. Let me see — yes, three metres high. Why, that's about twice as tall as you, Jesse."

Jesse jumped off the chair.

"This time," he said, "*Stevie* can be the mosquitoes."

What we were doing that day — that whole week, in fact — was helping Gertie get ready to audition for a big movie role. They're making a lot of movies in Vancouver these days. Gertie figured that if she could get a decent role in one of them, she could make "a few bucks to retire on."

We figured she had a pretty good chance. Back when she was younger, Gertie had been in lots of movies. She'd even lived in Hollywood. But lately she'd gotten a bit rusty.

Well, okay ... very rusty. Her last movie was in 1964.

Still, all she needed was a bit of practice. If only Jesse would co-operate ...

"What's your problem, Jesse? The mosquitoes are the stars of the movie, for crying out loud."

The movie was called *Slap*. It was about this swarm of mosquitoes that accidentally fly into a radioactive cave. The cave does something weird to them so they get bigger and bigger, until finally they're the size of office buildings. The whole time they're growing, they're looking for — you guessed it — human blood. At the end of the movie, they try to take over the world.

Jesse sat down on the floor, crossed his arms over his chest and stuck out his chin.

"Okay," I muttered. "Fine. *I'll* be the mosquitoes. You be Cissy Scanlon."

He looked up. "Cissy Scanlon? Dr. Kruger's wimpy assistant?"

"Right."

"The one who keeps pointing out the window at the mosquitoes? The one who keeps crying and screaming and fainting?"

"Right."

Jesse climbed back up onto the chair and got into a crouch. "*I'll* be the mosquitoes."

Gertie meanwhile was muttering away, running her fingers through her hair and making it stick up in little tufts. It was short and wiry and kind of two-toned — orange at the ends and grey at the roots. She said she was going to get it dyed before her audition. In the meantime, it was a perfect match for Freddy's tail feathers, which were poking out of an ivy plant.

Freddy the cockatoo wasn't crazy about me and Jesse. Every time we showed up, he disappeared into one of the zillion plants in Gertie's apartment. Gertie said he was just sulking, and we should ignore him.

"You know," she mumbled as she ruffled through the pages, "sometimes this whole script strikes me as kind of … well, foolish. If I didn't need the money so badly, I don't know that I'd bother." She rubbed hard at her nose — a round, stubby one without much shape. Gertie called it her "potato nose."

"Are you kidding?" I said. "It's going to be fantastic."

Jesse nodded. "I can hardly wait to see the special effects."

Gertie had told us that some of the effects would be done on computer. But they were also going to make a bunch of mechanical mosquitoes in five different sizes. The biggest ones would have eyeballs as big as satellite dishes, stingers the size of telephone poles. My skin itched, just thinking of it.

"I do wish the script were better," said Gertie. "Some of my lines are a little … well, silly."

Silly? Of course they were silly. You have to have *some* silly lines in a horror movie. That's when you get to take your hands off your eyes for a second to peek at the screen. If there weren't any silly lines, you'd spend the whole two hours with your jacket over your head.

I didn't bother explaining that to Gertie, though. I was in a hurry to get to the next part of the script. There was something special in it, something I couldn't wait to try.

For the next few minutes, the three of us read the script out loud. Gertie played Dr. Kruger, of course, and Jesse took the part of the mosquitoes. I played Cissy Scanlon.

Here's what we read:

Cissy: Dr. Kruger, what's happening? Why are the mosquitoes doing this?

Dr. Kruger: I don't know, Cissy. But as the world's foremost mosquito expert, I'm determined to find out.

(Cissy looks around nervously.)

Cissy: Gosh, Dr. Kruger, do you think we're in any danger? I mean, the mosquitoes have started to attack people, and they've been spotted in this area, and —

(Dr. Kruger pats Cissy on the shoulder.)

Dr. Kruger: Nonsense, Cissy. It's true that the mosquitoes have been sighted nearby, but that's no reason to — "

Mosquitoes:	Hummmmmmm …
Cissy:	What was that?
Dr. Kruger:	What was what?
Mosquitoes:	Hummmmmmm …
Cissy:	That! That humming noise.
Dr. Kruger:	That? That's just the refrigerator, my dear. Now, I have a theory about why the mosquitoes are suddenly behaving this way.
Cissy:	I've heard that some of them are getting as big as … as big as *people*, Dr. Kruger.

(Dr. Kruger chuckles.)

Dr. Kruger:	That's probably a huge exaggeration, Cissy. Why, no mosquito could possibly —

(The mosquitoes flap their wings.)

Mosquitoes:	Hummmmmmm …
Cissy:	There it is again. Did you hear it?

(Dr. Kruger stands, goes to fridge, opens and closes door.)

Dr. Kruger:	You see, Cissy? Just the refrigerator.
Cissy:	Oh, Dr. Kruger, it's such a relief to be around an expert at a time like this. People are saying

that the mosquitoes actually … *play* with their victims before they kill them.

Dr. Kruger: Play? Certainly not. The mosquitoes are quite serious. What they are doing, Cissy, is slapping.

Cissy: Slapping?

Dr. Kruger: Yes. You see, for thousands of years, we humans have been slapping mosquitoes. Just think how many you have slapped in your lifetime. It's my theory that the mosquitoes have finally begun to … well, resent this treatment.

Cissy: You mean … they're slapping back?

Dr. Kruger: Yes, Cissy. I think that what's happening here is … revenge!

Mosquitoes: Hummmmm …

(Cissy glances around wildly.)

Cissy: But, Dr. Kruger, if you're right, that means that the mosquitoes are capable of thought. It means that they can think and plan and —

Dr. Kruger: Quite so, quite so. We humans

have made a terrible mistake about mosquitoes. We have always assumed they are stupid. How wrong we were — how tragically wrong! Mosquitoes, Cissy, are among the most intelligent of all living creatures.

Cissy: Really, Dr. Kruger? Mosquitoes?

Dr. Kruger: Certainly, Cissy. They're —

(The mosquitoes become noisier.)

Mosquitoes: Hummmmmm …

(Cissy points at the window.)

Cissy: Dr. Kruger! Look!

THE MOSQUITOES, HUGE AND ANGRY, ARE AT THE WINDOW. THEIR EYES BULGE. THE HUM IS DEAFENING. THERE IS A FLASH OF MOSQUITO LEG. THE GLASS IN THE WINDOW SHATTERS.

CISSY LETS OUT A BLOOD-CURDLING SCREAM.

That was what I'd been waiting for. All my life, I'd wondered what "blood-curdling" meant. Loud, I guess. But how loud would a scream have to be to curdle blood?

I took a deep breath. Then another. I opened my mouth. I let out a screech that could curdle the blood of every man, woman and child for six blocks.

CHAPTER

GERTIE CLAPPED BOTH HANDS OVER HER EARS. Jesse and his chair wobbled back and forth before toppling to the floor with a horrible crash.

"STEE-VEE!" he yelled. "What are you doing?" Picking himself up, he rubbed hard at an elbow. Before I could answer, there was a frantic banging on the door.

It was Howard Biddlecombe, who lived next door — a scrawny guy with a pot belly and soft, droopy shoulders. The only interesting thing about him — and it was pretty interesting — was his hair. Okay, so lots of people have waves in their hair. Howard's had a *tidal* wave — a huge greasy swoop that crested about ten centimetres up and didn't settle down until way back behind his ears. He must have put some goop in it to make it stay that way. You could see the lines where he'd combed it.

"Gertie! Are you all right?"

"I'm fine, Howard." Gertie was thumping at her chest. "Stevie here got a little excited, that's all.

Just give me a second to catch my breath and make sure the old ticker's still working."

Howard and Jesse both glared.

I pointed at the script. "Look! It says right here. Blood-curdling scream!"

"Of course it does," said Gertie. "And a fine piece of acting it was, my dear. Very convincing." She gave her chest a final pat and smiled. "Maybe we ought to take a break. Howard, would you like to join us for a snack?"

A couple of minutes later we were all sitting around Gertie's kitchen table, drinking orange juice and munching on muffins. Gertie always bought the assorted pack from Mr. Muffin, and I managed to nab my favourite — Black Forest, full of cherries and chocolate. We were telling Howard all about *Slap*. He works at Goldy's Oldies, a video store that rents old classic movies, so he got really interested.

"My favourite part," I told him, "is when the mosquitoes attack the jumbo jet. There's this plane load of school kids on holiday, see? They're all having a great time, eating those little plane meals, colouring in those little plane colouring books? Little do they know that up there in the clouds, just waiting, are — "

"Fifty thousand huge, half-starved mosquitoes!" blurted Jesse.

I loved that scene. I had even drawn a picture of it and stuck it up by my bed. The plane was easy, but drawing all those mosquitoes nearly killed me.

Howard grinned and leaned forward eagerly. "Reminds me of a scene in *Brainsuckers from the*

Planet Zorb," he said. "You see, there's this … uh, yes, Jesse?"

Jesse was peering, cross-eyed, at Howard's chest. "Oh. I was looking at your pin, Howard. Is that a guitar?" Jesse had just started taking guitar lessons, so I guess that's why he noticed.

We all stared at Howard's chest. There it was — a little gold pin, shaped like a guitar, with a letter on each side. *E* and *F.* Howard held it up so we could see it better.

"It's the official badge of the Elvis Forever Club. We meet once a month — on a Tuesday." He paused for a moment, looking pleased. "I'm V.P. this year."

"V.P.?" repeated Jesse.

"Vice-president," said Howard proudly.

"Is it, like, a fan club or something?" I asked.

Howard nodded. Taking a tissue out of his pocket, he carefully polished the little guitar. "That's exactly what it is. A fan club. For Elvis Presley."

Now I was really confused. Didn't Howard *know?* "Howard," I said, as gently as possible, "Elvis is, uh, dead."

He stared back as if *I* was the one who was nuts. "Well, of course he's dead. He died on August 16, 1977. But his spirit? And his music? They'll never die, Stevie. Just as long as Elvis's music is played, the King of Rock and Roll lives on!" Howard lifted one hand, and for a second I was sure he was going to wipe away a tear. All he did, though, was rub the pin.

Jesse widened his eyes and shook his head slightly. I could tell we were thinking the same thing. Anybody who'd belong to a fan club for a singer who'd been dead all those years was definitely in nutso-cuckoo territory.

Howard smoothed a stray bit of hair into place. That's when I got it — Howard had Elvis hair! And right behind that brilliant thought came another.

"Hey, Howard, you know those people who go around imitating Elvis? Like, they have contests and dress up like Elvis and sing like Elvis and everything?"

"Elvis imitators!" said Gertie with a snort.

"Are you one of those guys?" I asked.

Howard shrugged. "I'd like to be. I mean, what could be finer than to follow in the footsteps of the King? But it's not an easy road, you know. You have to learn to play the guitar and memorize the words to all his songs and … well, I'm working on it. Getting pretty good, too. But I'm not ready for the big contests yet."

Gertie clattered the dishes together and carried them to the sink. "Honestly, Howard! Elvis imitator, indeed!"

"Gertie!" Howard looked hurt. "How can you say that? You, of all people. You, who met the King face to face."

"What???" said Jesse. "You met Elvis Presley?"

"She didn't just *meet* him," said Howard in a hushed voice. "She played in a movie with him."

"WHAT???" I yelled. Howard and Jesse jumped. Oops! Must have gotten blood-curdling again.

"What on earth is *wrong* with everyone?" muttered Gertie, as she rinsed the plates and cups. "All right. So I played Elvis's aunt in that movie —

oh, what was it called? Never mind, it was terribly silly. Elvis Presley was a nice, polite young man. Like … like Jesse here."

Jesse's eyes bugged out.

"And he had a lovely singing voice — just lovely," Gertie went on. "But all this nonsense since he died — people imitating him, seeing him everywhere, his picture in those supermarket magazines … well, it's ridiculous!"

Howard didn't look the slightest bit bothered by what Gertie said. In fact, he didn't even seem to be listening. His eyes got this wet little gleam in them, and when he spoke again, his voice was breathless.

"Gertie, do you suppose I could see … it? Just for a moment."

"Oh, Howard!" Gertie looked as annoyed as I'd ever seen her.

"Just two minutes, Gertie — I promise. I know how valuable it is."

It? Jesse and I stared at each other, confused.

"Pleeeeeeese," said Howard in a whiny little voice, just like a three-year-old. Jesse tried to hold the giggle in, but I could hear it.

"Oh, honestly," said Gertie. "This is the last time, Howard. The very last."

She headed into her bedroom, leaving me and Jesse alone with weird Howard. He stuffed his hands in his armpits, looked around the table and grinned. We could hear a door open and close, and then Gertie came back carrying a man's suit jacket.

But not just any jacket. It was pure gold — so

bright I actually had to squint when Gertie carried it into the sunlight. It looked steely hard and velvety soft — both at the same time — and it draped over Gertie's arm like a king's cape.

"Gosh!" said Jesse softly. "Is that real gold?"

"Pah!" Gertie gave the jacket a little shake. "Gold lamé, that's all. Just cloth. They made lots of these jackets back in the fifties."

"Oh, no they didn't," said Howard. "Not like *this* one." He touched the collar gently.

"What's so special about this one?" asked Jesse.

"It belonged to … him!" said Howard.

"You mean … Elvis Presley wore this jacket?" Jesse stared, pop-eyed.

Howard just nodded slowly.

"Wow!" I said. "Where'd you get it, Gertie?"

"He gave it to me."

"*He* gave it to you?"

"Yes, of course."

"Elvis Presley?"

"Great walloping dogfish!" shouted Gertie. "See what you started, Howard? The girl's besotted! Bedazzled! By a silly old fake-gold jacket!" She turned to Jesse. "You're too smart to get all star-struck, aren't you, Jesse?"

"Elvis Presley?" repeated Jesse in a squeaky little voice.

Gertie glared at him for a second. Then her mouth quivered at the edges and broke open into a huge Gertie laugh. Jesse grinned back and shrugged. Even Howard managed a little chuckle, although his eyes didn't move for one second off the jacket.

Gertie took off her glasses and wiped at her eyes. "Elvis Presley was a perfectly ordinary young man, doing his job — just like me if I get the part in *Slap*. There's no magic attached to this jacket, believe me."

"So why'd he give it to you?" asked Jesse.

"To keep me warm, of course! It was the end of a long day on the set, and I was wearing a sleeveless dress. Elvis noticed me shivering. He'd worn this jacket in a couple of scenes, and I guess he was through with it. Anyway, he put it over my shoulders and said, 'Keep it, Aunt Ida!' That was my name in the movie — Aunt Ida."

Howard sighed. "Just the sort of thing ... he ... would do."

"Hmmph!" said Gertie. "No more than any other decent person." She wagged a finger at Howard. "You listen to me, Howard Biddlecombe. You've been missing work because of this foolish club of yours. If you're not careful, you're going to lose your job. And who's going to get you another one? Elvis?"

Without another word, she stomped out of the room. Howard watched the jacket disappear. Then he wandered over to the door, all poky and dreamy.

"Thank Gertie for me," he mumbled as he left.

We tried to rehearse some more, but it was no use. Howard and the gold jacket had wrecked our concentration. Besides, it was getting awfully hot in the apartment. Gertie finally told Jesse and me we were off the hook.

"Go on down to the pool for your swim. Just be

sure to check in with me when you get back."

That's what was so neat about Gertie. "Keeping an eye" on us didn't mean that we had to stay right under her eyeball every single second. After we helped her with her acting each day, we were on our own — except for reporting in regularly. It was perfect.

Gertie walked us to the door and peered out into the hall. "Drat!" she said, looking in both directions. "I'm going to give that paper-boy a piece of my mind. That's five days now I haven't received a single newspaper."

"I know your paper-boy," said Jesse helpfully. "Mike Fischbein — he's in my class. Do you want me to call him and ask what happened?"

"Would you, Jesse? I truly do miss my morning paper. I like to read it with my lunch."

"We could go buy one for you," I offered.

"Not to worry," said Gertie, patting me on the back. "I'm going out for a walk later. I'll pick one up then. You two run along and have fun."

Jesse and I were almost at the stairs when we heard a strange sound. It was coming from Howard's apartment and sounded a bit like … crying? Was there something wrong with Howard? Putting a finger over my mouth to signal Jesse to be quiet, I crept up to the door and put my ear against it.

It *was* Howard. But he wasn't crying. He was playing the guitar and singing. At least, I *think* it was singing. Half screech, half wail — sounded like he'd gotten his toe caught in a lawn mower. I forced myself to listen. Something, something about a hound dog, and then:

> I ain't never got a jacket
> and you ain't no friend
> of mine.

Holding in a giggle, I ran back to Jesse.
"What is it, Stevie? What did you hear?"
I told him.
"That was 'Hound Dog,'" said Jesse. "It's an Elvis song. I have it in my guitar book — *Rock and Roll Favourites*. But you got the words wrong, Stevie. It's not 'jacket.' It's 'rabbit.'" And Jesse sang out loud — in that really nice singing voice I keep forgetting he has:

> You ain't never caught a rabbit
> And you ain't no friend
> of mine.

I shook my head. "You've got rabbits on the brain, Jesse. Must be that stupid day camp."
"It *is* rabbit," insisted Jesse. "Why would Elvis sing a song about a jacket?"
"Why not? He sang a song about his shoes, didn't he?"
"Oh. You mean 'Blue Suede Shoes.' Yeah, but — "
"No buts. It was jacket."
He shook his head. "Rabbit!"
"Jacket!"
"Rabbit!"

"This is stupid, Jesse. This is really childish."

"Rabbit, rabbit, rabbit."

I didn't say a word as we headed downstairs. I bit my lip as we crossed the courtyard. But as Jesse disappeared into his house to get his beach stuff, I couldn't hold it in any more.

"JACKET!" I yelled.

Blood-curdling.

CHAPTER

B Y THE TIME WE GOT TO KITSILANO POOL, WE'D forgotten all about rabbits and jackets and newspapers — everything on the planet, in fact, except cool blue water and hot summer sunshine.

Kits Pool is probably my favourite place in the whole world — a gigantic outdoor pool right beside the ocean. It has a shallow part for little kids, but Jesse and I always go to the deep end, where we can dive and race down the slides. From the top of the slides, you can see the high-rises of downtown Vancouver and the mountains behind them.

It took me thirty seconds, tops, to change my clothes and dive in. After that, I hardly even stuck my head up for the next five minutes. Fresh cool water all over my sticky skin and sweaty scalp … aaaaahhhhhh! When I finally surfaced, Jesse was beside me, floating on his back and staring up into the sky.

For the next hour, we only came out of the water long enough to jump back in. We dived to the bottom dozens of times, did somersaults, raced each other and cannon-balled off the side. On our last cannon-ball, a bald head popped out of the water at the exact same second that Jesse and I came down. We landed on either side of it.

So, okay, maybe we *were* a little close. Still, that was no reason for the lifeguard to yell that way.

"Hey, you two! The skinny kid and the kid with the hair. Watch it!"

The kid with the hair? I looked around. Everyone was staring at *me*. Totally insulted, I dragged myself out of the water. I couldn't believe it. Sure, I get a little frizzy in the pool. But … the kid with the hair?

Still grumbling, I followed Jesse over to the concession stand where we ordered curly fries and hot dogs — a tofu dog for Jesse, who's a vegetarian. We carried them over to a big log on the sandy beach.

The beach was packed, mostly with teenagers. Some of the guys were playing volleyball or Frisbee, but most of them were just lying around, showing off their muscles. The girls were lying around, too, covered in oils and creams. That's the funny thing about the teenagers at Kits Beach — they never get wet. A whole big ocean in front of them, and they just lie there, getting sweaty. I don't get it.

"Look!" Jesse pointed at a blanket. "Isn't that Fantasia?"

I looked. Yeah, that was her, all right. Fantasia Bayswater, a seventeen-year-old who lives in our co-op. She was lying on her back on a pale blue blanket, wearing the world's teeniest yellow bikini. Her hair was short and really blond, and her brown skin was greasy with sun-tan oil. Aside from the bikini, the only things she was wearing were sunglasses and a Walkman radio. Fantasia, I realized, is *always* wearing sunglasses and a Walkman radio — even in the middle of winter, even in the middle of the night. It's like they're welded onto her head.

We watched her for a few minutes.

"Is she breathing?" I asked Jesse. "Looks like she's dead." The smell of ripe strawberries drifted towards us — Fantasia's perfume.

"Huh," said Jesse.

"Like, I mean, when someone's lying down — even if they're sleeping — you usually see their chest move up and down. Or they give a little twitch now and then."

"Huh," said Jesse again.

I giggled. "I bet if you put a mirror under her nose, you wouldn't even get any steam on it. Do you think she's gone into one of those weird states like the yoga people do — where your heart goes really slow and you hardly even breathe?"

"Huh."

Jesse looked like he was in some kind of yoga state himself — except for his ears, which had turned this bright red colour, like somebody had squashed a couple of tomatoes on the sides of his head.

Wait a minute. Was it possible Jesse had a *crush* on Fantasia? I checked her out again. She *was* awfully pretty. If you like dead people.

"Hey, Jesse, do you *like* her?"

That got his attention. "Like who?"

"Fantasia, of course."

"Me? Fantasia? Are you crazy? She's seventeen, for crying out loud. I'm twelve. Me? Like her? Are you nuts?" His ears went from tomato to cherry.

"Okay, okay," I said. "Just asking."

"Well, don't ask, okay? She's seventeen. She's way taller than me."

"Okay," I said. "Let's drop it."

"Drop it? You started it in the first place. Me? Like Fantasia? Ha!"

We finished our lunch and headed home. By the time we got there, we were almost as hot as when we started out, so we went to my place and found a Blue Jays game on TV. There was a bag of fresh peaches in the kitchen, and we'd polished off about half of them when I remembered Gertie.

"Better check in," I said, dialling her number. After eight rings, I hung up.

"Probably gone out to buy a newspaper," said Jesse.

"Right." I flopped back down in front of the Jays. Spotting a hairbrush under the couch, I started pulling it through my tangled hair. I was still teed off at that lifeguard. Okay, so my hair's a bit bushy. So it goes a little nuts when it gets wet. Is that any reason to call a person names?

I gave a few more yanks and threw down the brush. No use. From now on, when I went to Kits Pool, people would point at me. "Pssst!" they would whisper. "It's the Kid with the Hair." I shuddered. Once you get a weird nickname, it can last your whole life. I could see myself — an old white-haired lady, hobbling into the pool on a cane. "Hey!" someone would yell. "There she goes! The Kid with the Hair!"

Rats!

The Blue Jays lost, and I didn't think about Gertie again until ten o'clock at night when my mom and dad and Jesse and I were watching the fireworks. Every August, fireworks teams from different countries have a big competition in Vancouver. The fireworks are set off on the other side of English Bay, but we live up on a hill, so we can see them really well from our top balcony. In the middle of a big green starburst, I glanced over at Gertie's apartment.

Dark.

"That's funny," I said.

"What's funny?" said my mom.

"Gertie said she was going to watch the fireworks tonight. She said she'd wave at me."

"So?"

"So she's not there. Her place is all dark."

"Well, maybe she's gone to bed," said my mom. "As people get older, they often fall asleep earlier. It's already happening to me."

For sure. My mom conks out at ridiculous times. Like right after dinner, she'll lie down on the couch "to glance through the paper" and end up snoring underneath it.

"Gertie's not like that," I said. "She's a night owl. She stays up till the middle of the night reading mysteries, like me."

"Maybe she had a long day," said my dad. "You two probably exhausted her."

"Wow!" Jesse pointed at the sky. "Will you look at that!"

We turned back to the fireworks, and I forgot about Gertie. Then I went to bed and forgot about Gertie some more. And the next morning, my mom and dad and I went to Galiano Island to visit some friends. I spent the weekend swimming and playing badminton and collecting rocks ... and forgot about Gertie the whole time.

It wasn't until Monday morning at nine — time for our next *Slap* rehearsal — that I remembered.

"Try again," said Jesse, after I'd knocked twice. "Maybe she's in the bathroom."

I knocked. Silence. At 10:35 a.m., when we came back, there was still no answer. Same thing at 1:20 p.m. By 3:45 p.m., we were starting to get worried.

"Maybe she's hurt," said Jesse. "Maybe she can't get to the door."

"Maybe we should yell to her."

Next thing you know, we were pounding on the door as hard as we could, bellowing "GER-TEEEE!" at the top of our lungs.

A door opened. Wrong door. It was Howard Biddlecombe, wearing a stiff white shirt with Goldy's Oldies on one pocket and the EF pin on the other. "What's going on out here?"

"It's Gertie," said Jesse. "Stevie and I have been knocking all day. Maybe something's wrong."

Howard shook his head. "Nothing's wrong. She's gone on holiday."

"What?" I squawked. "But ... she's got this big audition, and we're helping her and ... where did she go?"

"How do I know?" Howard was shifting from

one foot to the other. "A person has a right to go on a holiday."

"Did you talk to her before she left?" I asked. "What did she say?"

Howard frowned. "Nothing. I didn't see her." He started to close his door.

"Wait!" I said. "If you didn't see her, then how do you know she's on holiday?"

"The Pets Plus woman told me." He shut the door with a bang.

The Pets Plus woman?

I hammered on the door until Howard's face popped out again, flushed pink. Usually his skin is as white as his shirts — from all that time he spends watching videos, I guess.

"Who's the Pets Plus woman?" I asked.

Howard made a "tsk" sound with his teeth. "If you *must* know, Gertie hired someone to look after her plants and her cockatoo. People do that, you know, when they go on vacation. The company's called Pets Plus, and the woman was here this morning, watering the plants and feeding the bird." The door was closing again. This time I stuck my foot in the way.

"But why did she hire someone, Howard? Why didn't she just ask us? We'd have done it for free!"

Howard looked like he wished he had a giant broom, to sweep me and Jesse out of the building. "All I know is, she's gone! I don't know why. I don't know where. Frankly, it's none of my business. Or yours. Now, if you two *don't* mind, I'm busy!"

The slam made the whole hallway shake.

CHAPTER

5

JESSE LOOKED AS STUNNED AS I FELT.

"I don't get it," he said as we stepped into the sunshine of the courtyard. "Why wouldn't Gertie *tell* us she was going away?"

"Why would she go away at all? Her audition's on Saturday — only five days from now. She said she had a lot more rehearsing to do."

"And what about money?" added Jesse. Good point. Holidays cost money, and we knew Gertie was broke. That's why she was auditioning for *Slap*.

We flopped down on the grass under the Big Tree — a tall shady maple at the back of the courtyard — and just lay there, thinking. Something very weird was going on here. Something as weird as —

"Barbie and Ken?"

"What?"

"I said, wanna play Barbie and Ken?"

Standing in front of us was Tiffany, this little kid

who lives in the co-op. She was dressed in a tutu and her mother's high heels, and she was holding a basket with a checked cloth draped over it. A plastic leg stuck out the side.

"Oh," I said. "No … uh, thanks."

"Okay," said Tiffany cheerfully. She clip-clopped over to a flower bed on the other side of the courtyard and started singing in a high voice. "The wheels on the bus go round-and-round … " What was she doing? She had dug a long thin hole in the dirt and was laying a Barbie in it.

"There's something very strange going on here," I said.

"You're not kidding." Jesse was staring at Tiffany. "What *is* that — a Barbie funeral?"

"Not Tiffany. Gertie! There's something funny about her leaving. I can feel it in my bones."

"Uh-oh."

"What do you mean, uh-oh?"

"I know those bones of yours, Stevie. Whenever you feel something in *your* bones, I end up getting *my* bones broken."

This was an exaggeration. Okay, so a couple of times I'd dragged Jesse into just a teensy bit of danger. So we'd ended up in just the weensiest bit of trouble. But broken bones?

Not so far.

Tiffany was patting the dirt down over a Ken now, singing in a chirpy voice about the horn on the bus going honk-honk-honk.

"Maybe somebody *forced* Gertie to take a holiday," I said.

"People don't force you to take a holiday, Stevie.

That would be — "

I nodded.

"Oh, boy," he said.

I nodded again.

"Kidnapping? You're not serious!" He stared at me. Then, "You *are* serious."

He gnawed on a knuckle for a second, forehead all wrinkled. Over by the flower bed, the wipers on the bus were going swish-swish-swish as another Barbie bit the dirt.

Jesse shook his head. "Nah! No way! I mean, why would anybody kidnap a seventy-two-year-old woman with no money? Only rich people get kidnapped — for ransom."

He had a point.

"Besides, if someone did kidnap Gertie, wouldn't we have noticed something weird last week? Somebody phoning her maybe, or following her or — ?"

Something weird … something weird …

The newspapers!

"Something weird *did* happen, Jesse. Gertie's newspapers disappeared."

Jesse shrugged. "So? Mike Fischbein probably just messed up on his delivery route."

"Phone him." I pulled Jesse to his feet.

Mike Fischbein's mother answered the phone. She said Mike was out in the backyard, playing catch with his brother. It took ages for him to come to the phone so Jesse could ask about the missing papers.

"Uh-huh," said Jesse. "Uh-huh … uh-huh."

A long silence. Then, "Uh-huh."

"What's he saying?" I hissed.

Jesse shook his head. "Uh-huh ... yeah, uh-huh. I'll tell her."

After about ten more uh-huhs, he finally hung up.

"So?" I said.

"Mike says hi."

"To me?" I was surprised. "I don't even know Mike Fischbein."

"He saw us at the pool." Jesse looked embarrassed. "He said — are you sure you want to hear this? He said, say hi to the Kid with the Hair."

I groaned. I knew it! I was doomed! The nickname would spread — like a stain, like a blotch, like a horrible growth. I took a deep breath and clenched my teeth. Get a grip, Stevie, I told myself — this is no time to be thinking about your own problems.

"What about the newspapers?"

"They got stolen."

"Stolen!"

Jesse quickly reported what he'd learned on the phone. Mike, he said, was really upset because Gertie had phoned the newspaper to complain. Mike swore he'd left every single one of those newspapers right outside her door.

"Okay." I took a deep breath. "So what have we got here? Stolen newspapers. And now — "

Jesse gulped. "Stolen Gertie?"

A shiver slid down my spine. Slowly, I nodded.

"What about that pet service, Stevie? If someone grabbed Gertie, how would she have had time to hire Pets Plus?"

"She wouldn't!" I said. "She didn't! Someone else did."

Jesse looked at me blankly. "You mean ... the kidnappers? But why?"

"To throw us off the trail." It was all coming clear. "If anybody asks where Gertie is, the woman from the pet service will say she's on holiday. Right?"

Jesse nodded. "That's what she told Howard."

"So it's working, right? No one's suspicious."

"Except for us, of course."

"Right," I said. "So all we have to do is find out who hired the Pets Plus woman."

"Yeah," said Jesse, nodding again. "All we have to do is — what??"

"We'll interview her, the way the cops do in the movies, and then we'll — "

"Hold on a minute, Stevie. What do you mean, we?"

"You and me," I said. "Diamond & Kulniki. We can do it, Jesse. We're experienced detectives."

It was true. Even though we were only twelve years old, we already had a robbery and a smuggling under our belts. *Plus* I'd been reading mysteries practically since kindergarten. *Plus* I now had a new secret weapon. Movies! For the past six months, every video I'd rented had come from the mystery section. Columbo, Sherlock Holmes, Sam Spade, Alfred Hitchcock — anything with a crime in it. Stake-outs, surveillance, spying, tailing — I'd seen it all. And I hadn't just stuffed my face with popcorn and stared at the screen, either. No, I'd taken notes.

Jesse ought to know all this. He'd watched half the movies with me.

"Yeah, but, Stevie — "

"What?"

His eyes were wide. "If we're right, Gertie could be in real trouble. She could be sick or hurt or … you know … worse. This is serious, Stevie. We have to tell our parents."

It was like having ice water thrown over me. I knew what Jesse meant by … worse. "I guess so," I said. "There's just one problem."

"What's that?"

"Starts with an *s*, ends with an *s*, and has play dough in the middle."

Jesse swayed as if he'd been punched. "Sappy Rabbits!"

"If our parents find out that Gertie's gone away, we'll be holding hands to cross the street tomorrow!"

"Agghhhh!" Sticking a finger down his throat, Jesse pretended to gag.

"What if … we don't tell our parents?"

"What? Not tell them? Stevie — we can't. Gertie could be hurt or in danger … or … or worse."

Jesse was right, of course. The idea of worse got scarier all the time. But Sappy Rabbits was pretty scary, too. Jesse and I argued and talked and argued some more, but when my dad strolled into the courtyard at five, we still hadn't figured things out.

At dinner that night, the fried chicken tasted like sawdust. All I could think about was Gertie. Was she hungry? Was she warm enough? Okay, we were in the middle of a heat wave — she had to be warm enough. Maybe she was *too* warm?

Was she ... worse?

When Radical, my cat, brushed against my bare leg, I yelped. My parents stared. So did Radical, but his was a gimme-some-food stare.

"Something wrong, Stevie?" asked my mom, as I slipped a piece of chicken under the table to Radical. "You haven't said a word since we sat down."

"Wrong? Well, no. Not really."

"Not really?" My dad had a cob of corn halfway to his mouth, but he put it down again. "What does that mean?"

"It means ... well, sort of." I shrugged. "I guess ... you know ... a little bit."

My mom folded her hands on the table — a bad sign. "Okay, Stevie, what's going on?"

I looked around — at my mom, at my dad, and finally at Radical, who had fixed the old cat-eye on me again.

"Gertie's been kidnapped!"

"What???" They both said it at exactly the same time.

The next thing I knew, the whole day was spilling out like jigsaw pieces, all upside down and confused. "She wasn't there in the morning, and there was this woman from a pets place, but she hasn't got much money, and then her newspapers got stolen, but Fischbein told Jesse — "

"Whoa!" said my dad. "Slow down, Stevie."

So I told them the whole story, starting with the stolen newspapers and ending with Howard Biddlecombe slamming the door in our faces. By the time I finished, I was wiped out, but I knew I had done the right thing. Now all my parents had to do was phone the police.

Except they didn't.

My mom looked at my dad. "If Gertie's gone on vacation, we don't have a sitter."

"A what?" I squeaked.

"What about that day camp?" asked my dad. "Friendly Bears?"

"HAPPY RABBITS!" I yelled. "What about Gertie?"

"That's right — Happy Rabbits. Maybe they'd still have space for the rest of August."

"I don't know," said my mom. "It was getting pretty full when I phoned, and — "

"Haven't you two been LISTENING?" I interrupted. "I just told you — Gertie's disappeared! Gone! Vanished! A person disappears without a trace, and all you can think about is Happy Rabbits?"

My mom patted my hand. "Stop worrying, sweetheart. I've been telling Gertie for months she needs a break. She's the only one in the co-op who hasn't been away this summer."

"Yes, but — "

"She was complaining to me just last week about the heat. She was saying she'd love to get out of town."

"Yes, but — "

"I know you and Jesse have a lot of fun playing detective," said my dad. "But real life's just not that exciting. People *do* go on vacation without getting kidnapped."

"Jesse and I don't *play* detective!" I said. "We solved two genuine, actual crimes."

"And your dad and I are very proud of you," said my mom. "But what about all those not-so-genuine crimes?"

My dad began counting on his fingers. "Remember the thief who snuck into your room and stole two hundred valuable Superman comics?"

"Well, yeah." So, okay, nobody actually *stole* them. But somebody *did* move them to the storage closet — and it wasn't me.

"Remember when you decided that Annette Cloutier was a French spy?" said my mom. "You followed the poor woman around for weeks. She finally came to us to complain."

"And what about Dave Bilson?" My dad gave me a grumpy look. He was a little sensitive about Dave Bilson, who happens to be his boss. But as I explained at the time, it was a simple mistake. Could have happened to anyone. All I did was make a little phone call to the police.

"Dave Bilson looked *exactly* like the guy who robbed that Brinks truck in Winnipeg," I said. "If you'd seen his picture on *Crime Watch,* you would have turned him in, too."

"What your mom and I are trying to point out," said my dad, "is your tendency to invent mysteries where they don't exist. Maybe you're bored. Maybe some structured activities, like the ones at Happy Bears — "

"RABBITS!"

"Right. Rabbits. Maybe if you had more to do — "

"I have *plenty* to do."

"Stevie, we've been through this a hundred times," said my mom. "I just don't feel right about you and Jesse being on your own." She shook her head. "I just wish Gertie had let us know."

My dad shrugged. "Gertie's great with the kids, but I guess she's not too reliable."

"Gertie *is* reliable," I said. "She's been *kidnapped,* for crying out loud!"

My mom rolled her eyes.

That did it.

"Excuse me!" I said. A person can take only so many insults in one day. "If you're not going to believe me — "

"It's not that we don't believe you … "

But of course they didn't. As I headed for my room, they were already deciding who would call Happy Rabbits in the morning.

I cleared off a space on my bed and lay down. Were my mom and dad right? Was I simply the victim of an overactive imagination?

No. Something *was* fishy about Gertie's disappearance. I could feel it in my bones.

But now I was worse off than ever. Because now I had *two* problems:

1. How to find Gertie
2. How to keep Jesse and me out of the dumbest day camp in the history of the universe

The problem was — there was no way I could solve the second problem unless I solved the first problem, and there was no way to solve the first problem unless I solved the second problem.

See the problem?

Rats!

CHAPTER

6

NEXT MORNING, I FELT A BIT NERVOUS. TRUE, Jesse and I hadn't actually agreed to keep our mouths shut. But I'd heard my mom talking on the phone to his mom. Most of the conversation was really quiet, but I caught the only two words that mattered. Happy and Rabbits.

Jesse was waiting for me under the Big Tree. I was about to launch into a long explanation of how I *had* to tell, and then apologize for dragging him into Sappy Rabbits.

"I *had* to tell," he said, before I could speak. "Sorry I dragged you into Sappy Rabbits."

Dinner at the Kulniki house had been practically a copy of dinner at the Diamond house. "My mom acted like I was making it all up," said Jesse. "She told me Gertie's been talking about a holiday for a whole year now. She said Gertie was the 'spontaneous' type — whatever that means."

"It means you do things without planning," I told him. "Spontaneous" was the word my parents used when they changed my Saturday plans so we could go for a family hike. When I tried to change their plans, they called it "not thinking ahead."

Jesse picked up a pebble and tossed it into a bush. "She said something else, Stevie. She said maybe Gertie needed to get away … to work on *Slap* on her own."

Ouch. Now that was a pretty depressing idea. Was it possible that Gertie had left town to get away from *us?*

True, Jesse and I goofed around sometimes. Like my blood-curdling scream on Friday — it *did* end the rehearsal. Maybe Gertie was fed up with us. Maybe that scream was the last straw.

"Do *you* think that's what happened?" I asked Jesse.

"I don't know. No! If Gertie wanted to rehearse on her own, wouldn't she just tell us?"

I remembered how Gertie had stomped around her apartment, scolding Howard Biddlecombe about Elvis. Was this the kind of person who would sneak out of town to escape two kids?

"Gertie's in trouble," I said. "And if we don't help her, nobody else will."

It was true. Gertie's husband had died years ago, and she didn't have any children. She'd come from England when she was young, so she had no relatives around, either. All she had was her friends and neighbours. And *they* all thought she was in a lawn chair somewhere, drinking lemonade and rehearsing her lines.

"There's no way we can do any detecting in Sappy Rabbits, Stevie. We can't even cross the *street* in Sappy Rabbits."

"I know." What a horrible thought! Two

experienced detectives imprisoned in a kiddy camp.

"We'll have to work fast," I said. "Let's go check out Gertie's apartment. Maybe the Pets Plus woman is there right now."

We did.

She wasn't.

When I thought about it, our chances of knocking on Gertie's door just when the Pets Plus woman was there were pretty slim.

"She probably only comes once a day." I stared at Gertie's door. It was as flat and brown and boring as ever.

"Doesn't Gertie have any friends we could talk to?" asked Jesse.

I thought for a second. "Tonchia. Gertie and I went to visit her when she was sick. She lives about ten blocks from here."

We headed for our bikes.

❖ ❖ ❖

It was so hot we had to stop twice on the way to Tonchia's — once for a pop and once for an ice-cream sandwich. It was almost an hour before we finally stopped outside a tall green building with dark blue trim. The sign over the door said Carlisle Manor. Below that, smaller letters said Seniors' Residence.

"That's it?" asked Jesse.

"I think so. I wish I knew her last name."

Luckily, the receptionist knew. As soon as I said Tonchia, she pointed to an elevator. "Tonchia Balashnikoff," she said. "Apartment 401. She's expecting you."

We got into the elevator and pressed the button for the fourth floor.

"She's *expecting* us?" repeated Jesse. "What is she — a fortune-teller?"

The woman who opened the door of apartment 401 did look a bit like a fortune-teller. She was tiny, but her hair — snow white and piled up on top of her head — made her look bigger. She wore a black dress, a green tasselled shawl and funny little high-heeled shoes. Her dark eyes were shiny, and her mouth was round and purple, like a raspberry.

"Why so long?" she asked in a soft voice with a strange accent. "All morning I have been waiting for you."

Jesse and I were too surprised to speak. You see, I didn't really know Tonchia. When Gertie and I came to visit, the nurse had put Gertie's homemade chicken soup in the fridge and told us not to stay long. We'd barely poked our noses into the bedroom before the nurse shooed us out.

"Tch, never mind." Tonchia waved us in. "You are here now. What are you waiting for? Come in, children, come in."

The apartment looked like an antique store. Huge old stuffed couches, dark wooden wardrobes and cabinets, spindly tables with carved legs — all crammed in so close that there were only skinny little pathways left between. Jesse trailed Tonchia along one of these paths, and I followed. The curtains were pulled almost shut, probably to keep out the hot sun, but it made it hard to see.

Suddenly I heard a growl at my feet. It was a dog — about as big as my foot and totally covered in curly white hair. His teeth were bared in a ferocious snarl. A long strand of drool hung out one side of his mouth.

"Pushkin, no!" snapped Tonchia. "Down!"

Pushkin's lips relaxed back over his teeth. He looked really sorry he didn't get to bite me.

"Everything is waiting in the kitchen," said Tonchia. "I have a big box of glass bottles for you. Also a box full of cans."

Jesse glanced back at me, shaking his head in confusion. Tonchia grabbed his arm.

"Come, come," she said. "You can — "

She stopped and squeezed the arm. She squeezed lower, then higher — all the way up to his left shoulder in its white T-shirt. Finally, she grabbed his chin and pulled it down to her eye level.

"You're not a Girl Guide!"

"Uh ... no." Jesse's nose was practically touching hers.

"You're not even a girl!"

"Well, uh ... no." Jesse was looking *really* unhappy now.

"My glasses! Where are my glasses?" cried Tonchia, groping across the surface of a coffee table. Suddenly, she whirled, holding a cane above her head like a club.

"What do you want?" she demanded. "My jewels?"

"No!" squeaked Jesse.

"Pushkin!" she yelled. "Help!"

I don't know which attack school Pushkin went to, but he must have missed a few important lessons. Somehow he'd gotten the idea he should go for the *knees*. He started leaping straight up and down in front of me like he was on springs. Every time his teeth got close to my bare knees, he snapped. Dog spit sprayed my legs.

For a few seconds, I just stared. I mean, this was probably the dumbest dog on the planet. Finally, I stammered, "Wait! We're here about Gertie!"

Tonchia's arm came down a little. "Gertie?"

With a final desperate lunge, Pushkin sank his teeth into my left knee.

"Oww!" I yelled, mainly out of surprise. Pushkin's teeth weren't very big, and they weren't sharp enough to get a good grip. As we all watched, the little dog slid slowly down my bare leg. His teeth left a couple of thin scratches. Also a shiny trail of dog drool.

A smart dog would have given up, right?

Snarling with rage, Pushkin did a one-and-a-half-somersault flip and buried his teeth in the laces of my high-tops.

"Grrrrrrr-uff!"

No question about it — as a guard dog, he still had a long way to go. Meanwhile Tonchia's cane still hung like a sword over Jesse's head. If you ask me, Tonchia looked a *lot* more dangerous than Pushkin.

"Gertie's missing," blurted Jesse. "We're looking for her."

"Gertie? Missing?" Tonchia blinked. Slowly, she put down the cane. After a bit of peering and groping, she tracked down a pair of silver-framed glasses. She put them on, squinted at us and pointed to a wine-coloured couch.

"Sit!" she ordered. Jesse sat. I hobbled over, dragging Pushkin along like some kind of weird shoe ornament. There was drool all over my sneaker. I figured I might have to throw it away.

Tonchia sat across from us in a fat green chair with legs that ended in lion's paws. "So! You are not Girl Guides."

Jesse and I shook our heads. We were definitely not Girl Guides. It turned out Tonchia was expecting some Guides to pick up her stuff for recycling.

"And what is all this about Gertie?" Tonchia adjusted her glasses, then folded her hands in her lap. "Tell me. Everything!"

It took about twenty minutes. We could have told the whole story quicker, except that Jesse and I kept interrupting each other and Pushkin was making a lot of noise trying to chew his way through my shoe.

"So!" Tonchia said when we'd finished. She paused as if she was about to say something really important. Jesse and I leaned forward. "I will make tea. Yes?" She disappeared into the kitchen.

"Tea?" whispered Jesse. "It's a zillion degrees!"

"Never mind that," I whispered, waving Pushkin at him. "Help me!"

I had tried to shake the dog loose, but he was stuck on tighter than a leech. And now things were starting to get *really* gross — the spit had oozed through my sneaker and was sliming up the top of my foot.

Jesse grabbed Pushkin around his dog-waist.

"Hey! Look at that!" said Jesse, surprised. His hands around Pushkin's middle made such a tiny circle that his fingers overlapped. He flattened the hair along Pushkin's back. "There's hardly any *dog* in there."

"Rrrrrrr … " said Pushkin through his mouthful of laces.

Small or not, Pushkin wasn't easy to pull off. Jesse yanked so hard he lost his balance and fell over an end table. A framed picture clattered to the floor.

We looked around, alarmed, but there was no sign of Tonchia. I snatched up the picture. Luckily, the glass hadn't broken. It was a black-and-white photograph of two women, all dressed up with big fancy hats and — ugh! what was that? — dead animals around their necks. Some kind of weird fur collars. The two women were smiling, and behind them was this big building. Grauman's Chinese Theater, it said. I peered at the woman on the left. That nose! I'd recognize it anywhere. It was Gertie!

At the bottom of the picture it said *Tonchia and Gertrude, Hollywood, 1948*. Tonchia? I looked closely at the other woman. Yes! It *was* Tonchia, and, wow, had she ever been pretty.

"Here is poppy-seed cake, so good with lemon tea." Tonchia was backing into the room, carrying a tray. I put down the picture and darted to the couch. "Made especially for the Girl Guides — but

49

instead I serve it to Stevie and Jesse."

As Tonchia arranged the tea things, I looked at her closely. You could still see the prettiness — in those bright eyes and the softness of her skin. When Jesse and I both had tea in fancy flowered cups, she passed us fat slices of poppy-seed cake, running over at the edges with thick white icing.

"Eat!" she said, and waited till we'd each taken a bite. "I have been thinking about this story of a holiday. Children, you are right. Gertie did not breathe a word to me — her dearest friend — about such a holiday. Gertie did not have money for a holiday. My conclusion?"

We waited.

"I smell a mouse."

A mouse?

"Uh … do you mean a rat?" asked Jesse.

"Rat, mouse — it makes no difference." Tonchia waved a hand impatiently. "And now you must tell me — on which days were Gertie's newspapers stolen?"

"Every day last week," I told her. "Monday to Friday."

"Good, good, excellent. And now, children, you may stop worrying."

"But you just said you smelled a rat."

"Yes, but it is not for you to worry. You are children. Children can do nothing in matters of this sort. I, Tonchia Balashnikoff, will look after everything. I will — how do you say? — take over it from here?"

"Take over! Wait a minute. Jesse and I are — iiiiyy!"

Hot tea slopped out of my cup onto my hand. Jesse had done a big bounce at his end of the couch.

"Jesse!"

He shrugged. "Mosquito!" He slapped his leg hard, and the couch bounced again. More hot tea!

"Oww!" I said. "Cut it out! It's just a stupid mosquito!"

"Stupid? Ah, no." Tonchia's eyes narrowed, and her face got tight. Suddenly she was speaking with almost no accent. "We humans have made a terrible mistake about mosquitoes. We have always assumed they are stupid. How wrong we were — how tragically wrong! Mosquitoes, Jesse, are among the most intelligent of all living creatures."

It took me a second to remember where I'd heard that before. When I did, a little chill went through me. I glanced over at Jesse. He looked puzzled. Then his eyes widened as he got it.

"That's Gertie's speech," he said. "When she's playing Dr. Kruger in *Slap*."

"Gertie?" Tonchia shook her head. "No, no, Jesse. That role is wrong for Gertie, all wrong. I have told her so from the beginning. But for me, it is perfect." Her accent was back now.

"You mean," said Jesse, "*you're* auditioning for the role of Dr. Kruger, too?"

"Yes, yes, of course, I must audition — but it is only a formality. Ach, children, I was *born* to play that part. Dr. Kruger — it will be the crowning glory of my career." Clasping her hands, she took a deep breath, letting it out slowly in a long, heavy sigh. Her eyes behind the glasses looked blurry.

I jerked my head at Jesse, and he nodded. Detective language for let's-get-the-heck-out-of-here.

The knock made all three of us jump.

Jesse and I followed Tonchia to the door — the perfect opportunity to make a quick exit. As we threaded our way through the furniture paths, Pushkin was hot on our trail. He growled menacingly at my right shoe.

The door opened on blue uniforms, badges, gold pins — the works.

"We're here to — " one of the Guides began.

"But of course," said Tonchia. "Today every child in Kitsilano is coming to visit me. It is like Hallowe'en, yes? Come in, come in. We will have tea."

The Girl Guides looked confused but edged politely in the door. Jesse and I edged out.

"Wait!" Tonchia grabbed our arms. Pulling us close, she whispered, "I have some ideas."

Why was she whispering? Did the Girl Guides care? They were already inside, probably helping themselves to poppy-seed cake.

"You must not worry about Gertie, children." Tonchia's fingers dug into my arm. Her breath was hot on my cheek. "You play, you have fun. It is summer, yes? If I find something, I call you."

She backed slowly into her apartment. "I have some things I can do," she hissed. "I, Tonchia Balashnikoff, will take care of everything."

The door closed.

CHAPTER

7

A S SOON AS WE WERE IN THE ELEVATOR, JESSE started humming — the kind of music they play in movies when something creepy is about to happen.

"I, Count Draaaacula, will take care of everrrrything!" he said, raising his hands into claws above his head. My laugh came out louder than I expected — must have been the relief of getting away from Tonchia.

Wrapping both hands around his neck, Jesse made a strangled noise. "Aakkkkk! It was the poppy-seed cake!"

I grabbed my throat and fell to one knee. "Poisoned!" I gasped. "She got us!"

Next thing you knew, we were both writhing around on the elevator floor, moaning, "Poisoned, poppy-seed, aakkkkk, aakkkkk, aaakkkkk ... " It was so much fun, we didn't even notice when the door opened on the main floor. Who knows how long those two old guys stood there, watching?

I scrambled to my feet.

"Aaakkkk!" rattled Jesse from the floor. "Aaaakkk,

aaaaakkk, aaaakk."

I nudged him with my foot.

"Aaaaakkk … oh!"

As we ran out of the building, we really *were* choking — but from laughter. We had to walk our bikes to give ourselves a chance to calm down.

"What do you think?" Jesse asked finally.

"You mean Tonchia, the Queen of Weird? I think we told her way too much."

He nodded. "She seemed to want us to give up the case, Stevie. And she *really* wants the role of Dr. Kruger." He fiddled with his hand brake. "Do you think she wants it badly enough to … get Gertie out of the way?"

I jumped on my bike without answering. Gertie and Tonchia were best friends. Could a best friend do something like that? Even if she really, *really* wanted something? Could Jesse do that to me — or me to him? What if someone offered one of us a million dollars? A billion? Could we?

As I followed Jesse through Kitsilano, my mind was going in circles, but in the end, it always came back to the same place. The Pets Plus woman. *She* was the key. We had to talk to her — and soon. I pedalled harder.

Halfway home, Jesse braked so suddenly I almost ran into him.

"Oh, no!"

"What? What?"

"On the other side of the street," he said. "It's … them."

It was true. There they were — crossing the street. Yes, they were holding hands. And yes, they were wearing those goofy hats with the elastics under the chins. But that wasn't the worst part.

"Must be an art project," I said. "Oh, Jesse, this is way worse than I ever imagined."

"Tell me I'm seeing things."

The Sappy Rabbits must have spent the morning face-painting. Every one of them — even the leaders — had pink bunny noses and black bunny whiskers. Sticking out of the tops of their hats were these huge construction-paper ears. Bunny ears! Then one of them turned around.

"Tell me that's not a bunny tail." Jesse had one hand over his eyes. "I can't look … "

"It's a tail," I said between gritted teeth. "Looks like it's made out of cotton puffs."

"Do they all have tails?"

I watched the rest of the Sappy Rabbits cross the street.

"Some of them don't." The ones who didn't have tails had grumpy faces, probably from arguing with the leaders about the tails.

Any day, I thought … any day now, that could be me!

"If I have to walk around Kitsilano wearing whiskers and a tail," I said, "I'll die. I'll just die, that's all."

"They can bury us together," moaned Jesse. "Are they gone yet?" He peeked between his fingers.

We didn't say another word all the way home. Seeing those Sappy Rabbits was *very* scary. It made me want to start detecting twenty-four hours a day. As soon as we'd put our bikes away, we charged up to Gertie's apartment to see if the Pets Plus woman was there.

She wasn't. I thought back to the mystery movies I'd seen. "The only way we can be sure of catching her," I told Jesse, "is to sit here and watch the apartment — all day if we have to."

Jesse squinted, glancing from side to side like an undercover cop. "You mean ... a stake-out?"

"Right. A stake-out."

"We'll take it in shifts," he said. "That way both of us don't have to sit here the whole time. Who goes first?"

We flipped a coin, and I got the first two-hour shift. It was pretty boring, just sitting on the carpet at the end of the hall, waiting for someone to show up. I knew, though, from books and movies, that sometimes detective work is like this. Hours of doing nothing, waiting for a break.

Jesse took his shift, and then I did a second one. This time I was smart enough to bring along a library book — kind of a mystery, only creepier. It was called *The Thing in the Broom Closet*. I got about halfway through — to the part where the Thing was starting to come out every night at 4:00 a.m. All I can say is, it's a good thing that hall was brightly lit. Still, it was lonely and empty, with dark shadowy areas in the corners, and I was glad when Jesse came back for his second shift. He didn't have any luck either, and at five o'clock we packed it in.

Dinner that night was roast beef and potato salad — one of my favourite summer meals. Especially the potato salad. My dad makes it according to a Diamond family recipe that goes back hundreds of years — at least that's what *he* says. As far as I can tell, it has the same things as every other potato salad in the world — namely, potatoes, boiled eggs and mayonnaise. Except for … the secret ingredient! I can't say what it is, though, because it's a secret.

I mean, I'd *like* to … but I can't.

Oh, what the heck! It's pickle juice — that watery stuff that comes in the jar with the dill pickles. Makes dull old potato salad so delicious you end up sneaking bowls of it into your room in the middle of the night. Just a spoonful of pickle juice, though — two at most — or you'll end up with pickle soup.

Anyway, dinner. I was doing some serious eating when I noticed this odd smile on my mom's face — one of those smiles you get when someone's taking your picture and you *have* to smile.

"I called Happy Rabbits today, Stevie. Good news. They have room for you and Jesse starting next Monday."

My dad smiled a trying-hard smile, too. "Fantastic!" he said, smacking his hand on the table. "Boy, isn't that good luck."

I put down my fork. "Good luck?" I said. "Sure! Like a tarantula in your shoe is good luck!"

"Stevie — "

"Like a wasp flying up your nose is good luck!"

"Stevie — "

"I bet if a meteor fell out of the sky and landed on my head right this minute, you guys would say, 'Oh well, too bad about Stevie, but you know what? A meteor falling out of the sky is supposed to be *really* good luck!'"

"STEVIE!"

"What?"

My dad took a deep breath. "Okay. We know you're not crazy about Happy Rabbits. But we just can't leave you on your own all day."

My mom nodded. "I tried other day camps, sweetie, but everything else has been booked up since June."

I groaned. "Do you think maybe there's a *reason*, Mom? Why every other camp in the city is full and Happy Rabbits still has space?"

"It can't be that bad. Moira Lawson's daughter is going, and Moira says she's having a wonderful time."

"Mom! Zoe Lawson is six!"

"Try to see it our way," said my dad. "We have to be sure you're safe."

"Try to see it *my* way," I said. "I'm the one who's going to end up with giant ears sticking out of my head."

"Okay, okay," said my dad. "If you can come up with an alternative, we'd be glad to listen. If you can't, it's Happy Bears, er, Rabbits."

An alternative! Now there was an idea. Who else around the co-op could supervise me and Jesse until we found Gertie? Most of the adults were on holiday or working. The rest had little wee kids and spent a lot of time at playgrounds and kiddy pools. That would be almost as bad as Happy Rabbits.

Wait a minute — there *was* someone!

"Fantasia Bayswater!" I said. "She's around during the day. She's not exactly an adult, but she's the same age as the leaders in Happy Rabbits." It was true. The Happy Rabbits leaders were mostly older teenagers.

My mom looked horrified. "Not in a million years!"

"Why not? I mean, we could report to her regularly, and if there was an emergency, we could — "

"I wouldn't trust her with my pet cat."

Radical glanced up, half-asleep, from the corner.

"What's wrong with Fantasia?" I asked. I mean, sure, she didn't *do* much and she spent most of her time just lying around, but that should make her a perfect supervisor.

"She's self-absorbed, irresponsible, disrespectful and rude." My mom's head bobbed sharply after every word.

"Rude?" Fantasia hardly opened her mouth. All she ever did was listen to her Walkman.

"Any seventeen-year-old who would yell and swear at a senior citizen is definitely rude!" said my mom.

"What???"

"Last Friday afternoon," she said, "Amy Minelli from 406 was walking past the laundry room when she heard this terrible racket. People fighting. Amy didn't catch it all, but she did hear some pretty awful language. So she opened the door, and who did she find?"

"Who?"

"Fantasia Bayswater, that's who — yelling at poor Gertie Wiggins. She had Gertie backed right into a corner. Of course when Amy came along, Fantasia stopped shouting and ran off. But can you imagine? What on earth got into the girl?"

Exactly what I was wondering.

"What was Fantasia yelling about?"

My mom shrugged. "Gertie wouldn't say."

"But ... what did Gertie do then?" If this argument happened on Friday afternoon, what Gertie did next could be really important. "Did she go home? Did she go out? Did she — "

"I don't know," said my mom. "What does it matter? The point is, your dad and I want you to be safe while we're at work. Fantasia is out of the question. And if nobody has any other ideas, well ... Happy Rabbits is the best we can do."

"Maybe it's just the *name* you don't like," said my dad. "It's kind of a dumb name. Maybe if we called it — I don't know — the Cool Dudes Camp or something ... "

I gave him a look. Was he serious?

"Okay, maybe not," he said. "But let's talk about this. What — "

"Dad! I'd love to talk. Maybe later. Right now I have to go see Jesse!" Wait till he heard about the fight in the laundry room.

"Aren't you forgetting something?" My mom nodded at the dirty dinner dishes.

The dishwasher was jammed with clean dishes that all had to be put away before I could even start loading. And then there were the pots that had to be scrubbed. And *then*, when I was finally finished, my dad remembered the hall closet, which I had promised to tidy three days ago.

(This, by the way, is the story of my life, and the reason why I have only solved two mysteries so far instead of twenty. Does Nancy Drew do chores? Think about it.)

By the time I got to Jesse's, it was after seven.

"He's baby-sitting Alexander," said his mom.

Rats! I'd forgotten. Alexander is this five-year-old kid that Jesse and I both baby-sit. Jesse had a regular job there every Tuesday night while Alexander's mom went to pottery class.

"Tell him I need to see him," I said. "Tell him it's really urgent!"

"Sure, Stevie." Marcia Kulniki smiled. "Isn't it good news about Happy Rabbits?"

Right, I thought. Like a wasp up your nose is good news, like a tarantula in your shoe … oh, what was the point?

"Sure," I muttered. "Great news."

I slumped back home, hoping I could at least find something decent on TV. A mystery maybe? I brightened. But my parents were glued to their chairs for a two-hour special. *Parenting Your Pre-Teen Child: The Challenge.*

"It's just started, Stevie. Want to watch?"

I'd rather watch lint gather in my belly button.

Shaking my head no, I headed for my room. What a useless, crummy evening. Here I had this exciting new information about the case, and where was my partner? Off doing nothing — or practically nothing. Alexander's mom always rented some terrific new video and left tons of snacks for the baby-sitter. You hardly had to get off the couch all evening except to fill the chip bowl.

Okay. Fine. I'd just have to figure things out on my own. Why, for starters, would Fantasia yell and swear at Gertie? What had made her so angry? And exactly how angry was she? Angry enough to do something more? Something … worse?

It was time, I decided, to do what I've done on other cases — make a suspect list. I ransacked my bedroom and finally found an old Grade 3 journal in my sock drawer. I ripped a page out of the back and wrote in my best handwriting:

GERTIE WIGGINS, MISSING PERSON

I read it over twice. Looked good. Leaving a couple of spaces, I added:

LIST OF SUSPECTS
1. TONCHIA BALASHNIKOFF — WANTS MOVIE ROLE
2. FANTASIA BAYSWATER — VERY ANGRY! WHY?

Underneath that, I wrote:

CLUES:
1. STOLEN NEWSPAPERS
2. WOMAN HIRED FROM PETS PLUS

I studied the list for a long time, hoping for a brilliant idea.

Brilliant ideas are like detecting partners — never there when you need them.

At nine o'clock, I gave up and went to bed.

Maybe if I got to sleep early, I could *dream* a brilliant idea? But the moment I was curled up in my bunk, I remembered *The Thing in the Broom Closet*. I'd gotten to this really exciting part, where the Thing was pushing its slimy green tentacles across the floor of the girl's room, creeping, creeping, while she slept ...

At 1:30 a.m., I was still reading. How could I leave her there with that Thing crawling around her house? I *had* to finish. Well, they caught the Thing, of course. In fact, they caught it a couple of times. (The first time, it slimed right out of its cage. Served them right. Why would anyone put a Thing made out of jelly-slime into a *cage?*) Eventually, they discovered the one thing that would dissolve it — root beer. I'm not kidding. They poured root beer all over it, and it shrivelled right up, like the witch in *The Wizard of Oz*.

As soon as it was shrivelled, I turned the light out.

And lay there.

Listening.

What kind of noise would a jelly-slime make?

Shadows flickered across the room. Maybe the wind. Maybe not. I wished I had a bottle of root beer.

All I could find in the fridge was half a bottle of ginger ale. Okay, maybe it was stupid, but it made me feel better — stuffing it under my pillow. Not that I really expected anything to happen. I mean, it was only a book ...

By the time I finally drifted off, it was close to 2:00 a.m.

CHAPTER

8

I WOKE UP TO A BLAST OF SUNLIGHT AND THE SMELL OF something frying. Two minutes to ten! Why hadn't someone woken me up? And an even better question — who was in the kitchen? My parents both left the house by eight-thirty.

As I crept down the stairs, I couldn't help thinking about *The Thing in the Broom Closet*. Not that I really expected the Thing to be in my kitchen, frying up breakfast. Still …

"Hey there, Rip Van Winkle!" said my mom. "How about pancakes?"

"What are you doing here, Mom?"

"Oh, I guess I'm feeling a little guilty about leaving you on your own so much. I thought we could have a leisurely breakfast together."

A leisurely breakfast? Today? When I had so much to do?

"Listen, Mom, I — "

"You sit right down and dig in. Strawberry syrup or maple?"

"Maple. Mom, I — "

"There's bacon, too."

Bacon? Well, maybe I *could* hang around, just for a while.

We played a quick game of Pam's Place while I ate. That's where my mom pretends to be Pam, a TV interviewer, and I pretend to be famous people she's interviewing. Must have had Howard Biddlecombe on the brain because I chose Elvis Presley. Problem was, I didn't know much about him. Except that he was dead.

"How did you get to be so famous?" asked Pam.

"I, uh, died."

"Oh," said Pam. "Well, then, tell me about your home — Graceland."

Graceland?

"It's, um … pretty dead there."

"Pssst! Stevie!" Jesse was at the window, motioning me outside.

"See you later, Pam — I mean Mom." My lips missed her cheek as I ran by.

"Wait till you hear!" I said to Jesse as soon as we were settled under the Big Tree.

"No! Wait till *you* hear!" Jesse's grin was as wide as his face. "I talked to the Pets Plus woman!"

"You did? When?"

"This morning."

"Jesseeeeeeee! Why didn't you call me?" I couldn't believe it. The whole time I'd been stuffing down pancakes and bacon, he'd been interviewing our prime witness.

"I came by your house early this morning, Stevie, but your mom wanted to let you sleep in."

"And you *listened* to her?"

"I didn't even know the Pets Plus woman would

be there, Stevie. What was I supposed to do when she opened the door? Ask her to wait while I went and got my partner?"

"Yes," I said, "but never mind. Tell me. Everything!"

Jesse took a deep breath and started rattling it off. "Eight-fifteen a.m., I get up. I get dressed, then I eat my usual breakfast — granola with bananas and milk and a glass of orange juice. I say goodbye to my mom, who leaves for work at approximately eight thirty-five. I clean up my breakfast dishes, which takes me to approximately eight forty-five. So at eight-fifty, I'm — "

"Uh, Jesse? Can you just skip to the part where you talk to the Pets Plus woman?"

He looked hurt. "I was getting to that, Stevie. Detail is important in detective work."

"Okay, okay. What happened next?"

"At eighty-fifty, I'm standing outside Gertie's door, knocking. So the door opens and this woman is standing there holding a watering can."

"What did she look like?"

"Ordinary."

I waited, but he didn't add any more. "What else?"

"Just a regular, ordinary woman, Stevie."

"Jesse! You just finished telling me how important detail is."

"She didn't have any detail."

Was he *trying* to drive me nuts?

"Was she tall? Short? Fat? Thin? Dark? Blond? Old? Young? Any distinguishing marks or scars?"

Jesse shrugged. "Medium tall. Medium fat. Medium hair. Medium age. Like I said, ordinary."

"Okay, okay. Just tell me what she said."

"Well, she was the Pets Plus woman all right. It was written right on her shirt. But she wouldn't answer any questions. She says it's Pets Plus policy not to talk about their customers. And you know what was really weird? *She* was acting suspicious of *me*."

"What do you mean?"

"She asked me why I wanted to know. Said there'd been a wave of robberies around here. Like I was a thief or something! Like I came there to rob Gertie's apartment." Jesse looked really insulted.

"Well, a lot of break-ins happen when people are away on holiday. And lots of the thieves are teenagers." I'd heard my mom and dad talking about this.

"I'm not a teenager," said Jesse.

"Well, *she* doesn't know that." But looking at Jesse, I just couldn't see it. Would a house-robber have braces on his teeth? Would a house-robber wear a big yellow badge that said Superman Lives?

"Wait a minute, Stevie. I do remember a detail. She had an English accent." He looked so pleased that I hated to hurt his feelings. It was a pretty crummy detail, though. Lots of people in Vancouver have English accents.

"Well, that's good, Jesse. That's — " I stopped. He was staring over my left shoulder. Both his ears were turning pink. I turned to look.

Fantasia. She was dressed all in black, her shorts and little halter top made out of that stretchy stuff that clings. As she strolled through the courtyard, she hummed — probably the song on her Walkman. Her face was so blank it was hard to imagine her angry. She disappeared into her town house, leaving the smell of ripe strawberries floating in the air.

"Wait till you hear what *I* found out!" Quickly, I told Jesse the story of the fight between Gertie and Fantasia.

"Fantasia *yelled* at Gertie? Swear words? In the laundry room?" Jesse groaned.

I knew just how he felt. Back in Grade 5, I had a crush on this really cute boy named Jason. Then one recess I saw him stealing a kindergartener's potato chips. He didn't even eat them — he just scrunched up the whole bag and threw it in a puddle. I couldn't believe it. How could someone who looked so good act so rotten?

When you think about it, though, why not? Why should cute people be nice? If anything, it should be the other way around, right? I mean, the cute people —

"Stevie! Are you listening?"

"What?"

"I was saying that things are getting complicated. Maybe we should make a list of suspects."

"Already did that," I said. "Wait here."

I ran into my house and grabbed the suspect list. I was almost out the door when the phone rang.

Tonchia.

"Stevie? It is I, Tonchia Balashnikoff. You must come for lunch today — you and the boy, Jesse. The Pacific Grand Hotel. You know where it is?"

"Uh, yeah." Downtown. Really fancy.

"Good! You will meet me there at twelve o'clock. The Versailles Room — it is the best, yes? I pay for everything — food, drink, everything!"

"But … why?"

"I have important news. We must talk. See you at — how do you say? — twelve o'clock pointed!"

"Pointed? Oh. You mean sharp."

"Pointed, sharp — it makes no difference. You will be there, yes? Goodbye."

"Wait — "

Click!

What was *that* all about? If Tonchia had news about Gertie, why couldn't she just tell me on the phone?

Jesse made a face when I told him.

"Well, at least we're meeting her in a big public place," I said. "A least there'll be two of us."

"Uh, not exactly. I have a guitar lesson at twelve."

"A guitar lesson? Jesse!"

He shrugged helplessly. "My mom already paid for it."

"You expect me to meet the Queen of Weird all by myself?"

"It's a big public restaurant, right? And she's little and old, right? And you're bigger and stronger, right?"

Right. Right. Right.

"What's she going to do? Throw a bread roll at you?"

"Okay," I muttered. "I'll go already. I'll go alone."

It was just lunch, right?

What could happen?

❖ ❖ ❖

"Yes?" The waiter at the Versailles Room was wearing a bright white shirt, a black bow-tie and a very unfriendly expression.

Maybe it was my clothes. Maybe the Versailles Room didn't get a lot of twelve-year-olds in faded blue jeans and sneakers with dried dog-spit on them.

"I'm, uh, meeting someone. Tonchia Balashnikoff."

He checked a big black book on his high wooden desk. Then he nodded. "We have a reservation. Follow me please."

I did — across a huge room with chandeliers hanging from the ceiling and stone fireplaces in the walls. The tables had pink tablecloths with vases of red roses and white cloth napkins. Most of the people were all dressed up and talking so quietly you could hear their forks clink against their plates. A couple of them looked up, surprised, as I walked by. Maybe I should have brushed my hair.

The waiter led me to a little table beside the wall with plates and silverware for two. I was starting to think he wasn't so bad after all, when he tried to pull my chair out from under me. Just as I went to sit down — whoosh! — it slid backwards. If I hadn't grabbed it at the last minute, I would have landed on my backside.

"Hey!" I muttered.

He rolled his eyes. "I am seating you, miss."

Try seating me in a *seat*, I thought.

He handed me a menu as big as the table and left. Most of the stuff on it I'd never heard of — radicchio, endive, gorgonzola, almondine. Where were the burgers?

And where was Tonchia? I checked out the table beside me. A guy in a white suit was pulling a crab apart. Across from him, a blond woman picked at a scruffy-looking salad with pieces of tangerine on top.

"May I take your order, miss?" Another waiter, practically a twin of the first one, except his hair was parted in the middle.

"I'm, uh, waiting for someone."

Fifteen minutes later, I was still waiting. The crab-and-salad people had been replaced by three guys in grey suits — a little bald, half-bald and totally bald. When Totally Bald saw me, his eyebrows shot up. You could see him wondering what this kid was doing all by herself in the most expensive restaurant in Vancouver.

Good question.

Where the heck was Tonchia, anyway?

The waiter came by for the third time. He didn't say anything, but I could tell it was time to order. I opened the menu again. Better find something I could pay for, in case Tonchia didn't show up at all. In my wallet was five dollars and change.

I pointed at the only thing on the menu that was under five dollars.

"The *chèvre*. Very good, miss. And?"

"And what?"

"Something to drink?"

"Oh." I thought hard. "A glass of water, please."

"Water?"

"Ice water."

"Very good, miss. *Chèvre*. With ice water."

"A tall glass," I added.

"Tall," he said.

"With lemon."

"Lemon." He closed his book.

A few minutes later, he was back with a plate. On it was something that looked like a fried yellow hockey puck.

"Uh … what's that?"

"*Chèvre*."

It stunk like —

"Goat cheese, miss."

I stared at it. "You're kidding me. Right?"

Eyes half closed, he shook his head.

Perfect! A hundred choices on the menu, and I'd ordered a lump of fried goat cheese.

"Hey, uh, listen, maybe — "

But he was gone. I sighed. This was quickly becoming the worst lunch of my life.

The hockey puck was mushy inside and tasted like an old sock. By chewing slowly, I managed to stretch it out for forty-five minutes. At one o'clock, I had to face facts. Tonchia wasn't coming.

I paid the waiter his five bucks and left, feeling pretty, um, cheesed off. In some places, you can get a whole *pizza* for five bucks! On the bus home, I got madder every minute. Why would

Tonchia do something like that — invite me to a fancy restaurant and not show up?

There were two messages waiting on the phone machine. Maybe Tonchia, calling to say why she couldn't come? Maybe an apology from Jesse? I pressed Play.

"Mrs. Diamond? It's Tammy from Happy Rabbits! Guess what? Stevie and Jesse won't have to wait till next week to join our summer adventures. We have two spaces available starting tomorrow! Isn't that super? If you want them, give me a buzz before five tonight. Or Stevie? Why don't *you* call? We can get to know each other!"

Ha! In your dreams!

The next message started with a funny clunking noise. It was followed by a soft whispery voice. "Stevie? Are you there?"

My heart stopped.

"Pick up the phone."

I knew that voice.

"I only have a minute to talk. I — "

Clunk, clunk again. Then a garbled, muffled sound. Then a dial tone.

Gertie!

73

CHAPTER

IT TOOK AT LEAST A MINUTE BEFORE I COULD GET MY finger to press Play again. Gertie's voice was quick, almost whispery. Why? And why did the call end so suddenly?

I listened a third time. Jesse and I were right. Gertie *was* in trouble! Why else would she sound so strange on the phone?

Suddenly — almost like a movie — I could picture the whole thing in my mind. A Mysterious Someone had captured Gertie and was holding her prisoner. But Gertie was smart — she'd be watching, waiting for her chance. Today, for just a second, she gets her hands on a phone. Quickly she dials, her eyes darting around nervously. Who does she phone? The one person she knows who's experienced in criminal detection — me! She's frightened; she talks quickly and in a whisper. Just as she's about to tell me where she is, the Mysterious Someone comes in and … catches her! Gertie drops the phone — clunk, clunk. The Mysterious Someone grabs it away and hangs up — click!

Could it really have happened like this? I listened to the message again, fast-forwarding past the Happy Rabbits message. Yes. I was positive. And now I had solid evidence. Once my parents heard this tape, they'd *have* to believe Gertie was in trouble.

But wait a minute. Big problem. If I played Gertie's message for my parents, they'd hear Tammy's message, too. They'd phone her back quicker than you can say Sappy Rabbits Stupid Adventures. By nine o'clock tomorrow morning, Jesse and I would be cutting out bunny ears.

Unless ... maybe I could erase Tammy's message but still leave Gertie's. Now where was the manual that went with the answering machine? I rummaged around in the kitchen drawers, found it under some tea towels and skimmed through the directions.

The way I had it figured, you'd press Play first. Then, when you got to the end of the first message, you'd quickly press Rewind. Then you'd press Erase Message, then Rewind again.

I did it. When I was finished, I pressed Play again to hear Gertie's message.

Sssssssssssssssssssssssssssssss ... the hiss lasted about thirty seconds, then stopped. The tape rewound. Click.

Silence.

I tried again. Play, I begged, please Play.

I waited. Nothing. Just the hiss.

I tried again. Nothing.

I'd lost Gertie on the tape!

How could I *do* something so stupid? I stomped

around the house, slamming doors and calling myself names. "You idiot! You mush brain! You nincompoop!" Storming into my bedroom, I spotted an old stuffed rabbit lying on the floor. A rabbit! With one swift soccer kick, I booted it halfway across the room. It bounced off the wall and landed in the fish tank. Radical took one look and scrambled under the bed.

Fishing the soggy rabbit out of the tank calmed me down a bit. My next move, I figured, was to phone Tonchia. Maybe her "important information" had something to do with Gertie's call.

No luck. After ten rings, I hung up and headed over to Jesse's. As I ran up the steps to his house, Tiffany rolled by on a tiny two-wheeled bicycle. "He's not home, Stevie. He's hiding in the bushes."

"He's what?"

"In the bushes. Across the street."

I followed her to the front gate, where she pointed at this thick hedge in the little park across the street. If you looked really closely, you could see splotches of red T-shirt in the middle of the green. I crossed over and peered into the hedge.

"Jesse? Are you in there?"

From out of the bush came a hissing sound. "Sssshhhhhhh!"

"Come on out. I have to talk to you."

The hedge came alive, swaying and jiggling, all its leaves and branches trembling. A few seconds later, Jesse crawled out, twigs clinging to his clothes and hair.

"Quiet, Stevie. I have a suspect under surveillance."

"A what?"

"Follow me, and keep your head down."

The hedge was up to our shoulders — one of those bushy ones the park people trim so they have flat sides and tops. After a lot of grunting and struggling, we pushed our way through to an empty spot in the middle — a perfect hiding place. Jesse pointed through the branches.

"Look!"

On the grass in front of us was a large white blanket. Fantasia Bayswater lay on it, wearing her usual outfit — bikini, sunglasses and a Walkman. Beside her was a package of potato chips, a magazine and a blue beach bag. She was moving at her usual speed. In other words, not at all.

"I figured since she's one of our prime suspects, I'd better keep an eye on her." Jesse's ears were a pale raspberry colour.

"Never mind her," I said. "Something really important has happened. I just talked to Gertie!"

"You WHAT???" he yelled, easily loud enough to reach Fantasia's blanket. I peered nervously through the hedge. It was okay — she couldn't hear a thing with that Walkman on.

"Well ... I didn't exactly *talk* to her. But I did hear her voice." I told him about the phone message.

"Great! Let's go listen." He was already climbing out of the hedge.

"Well, we, uh, can't." So then I had to explain the whole tape-erasing disaster.

"I can't believe it. You erased the tape? Stevie, you destroyed our only evidence!"

"Don't you think I *know* that? I'm a rotten detective, okay? I should be thrown off the case — okay, already?"

"Sheesh, Stevie, you don't have to be so touchy."

I shifted around, untangling my hair from a branch and trying to find a less scratchy place to sit. Hedges make good hide-outs, but they're not exactly comfy.

"What happened at your lunch with Tonchia?" Jesse asked.

I told him about the fried hockey puck.

He nodded sympathetically. "Maybe we should phone her."

"Already did. She's not there."

"So what now?"

"So nothing," I said glumly. "Tonchia's not home. Gertie's phone message is destroyed. The Pets Plus woman won't tell us anything. Everywhere you look — dead ends."

"Not quite." A sly little smile curled up the sides of Jesse's mouth. "Fantasia's a suspect, too, don't forget. And I've had her under constant surveillance since she came out of her house."

"So?"

"So she's been acting really strange, Stevie. Like, she's lying there, and she's reading her magazine, see? And all of a sudden she gets so mad, she makes a fist and pounds it."

I gawked. "She *punched* her magazine?"

"Yeah! I know it sounds weird, but that's not all. Next, she reaches into her bag and brings out this big felt marker. All of a sudden, she's scribbling all over the page."

"Scribbling what?"

He shrugged. "I couldn't see from here."

Fantasia hadn't moved. She was kind of like a slug, I figured. The fastest she ever moved was about ten centimetres an hour.

"We have to get a look at that magazine," I said.

Jesse gulped. "I was afraid you were going to say that. But how?"

Good question. Fantasia *did* have her back to us. And she *was* pretty dozy. Still, there was no way we could just waltz up to her blanket and help ourselves to her magazine.

A minute later, I had it. "Water bombs."

"What?"

"If we throw water bombs at her, she'll *have* to get up. I mean, she probably won't move fast, but at least she'll get off the blanket."

"And then what?"

"Then I'll stick my head up so she can see I threw the bomb. Then I'll run away, and she'll chase me. And then *you'll* look at the magazine."

There was a pause. "What if she catches you?"

"Are you kidding? The Slug Princess?" I just happen to be the fastest kid on the whole track team. No way in a million years Fantasia was going to catch me.

"Sounds a little risky."

"Trust me," I said. "Wait here. I'll get the water bombs."

Ten minutes later, I was back. After wriggling my way back into the hedge, I handed Jesse two of the four balloons I'd filled with icy water.

"Hold these for me. I'll probably just need one."

"I don't know, Stevie. I — "

"Here goes." I stood up straight so my arm would clear the hedge. With my best overhand baseball throw, I hurled the balloon as hard as I could at her blanket. Then I ducked and peered through the branches.

Sploosh! The balloon landed with a wet smack on the grass about half a metre in front of Fantasia. Some of the water must have got her because she lifted her head slowly and glanced around in surprise. Then she lay back down in slug position.

Oh well, I'd get her with number two.

"Stevie, wait!" said Jesse. "I can't see."

I stood up again, high enough to get a good view. Tiffany and this little boy named Benjamin were standing right in front of the hedge, but they were busy comparing bicycle horns and didn't see me. The Slug Princess was still lying there, not a muscle moving. I raised the second balloon, threw and ducked!

Total silence.

Rats!

"Did you hit her?" asked Jesse.

"I don't know."

That's when Jesse made his fatal mistake.

"No," I whispered as he popped his head up. "Wait!"

Tiffany's voice was clear and tinkly. "It was Jesse, Fantasia. He threw it. See? There he is, in the bush."

"NO!" hollered Jesse. "No, I — iiiiiiiiiiiiii!" It was

like an explosion. Thrashing, twisting, punching, kicking, Jesse ripped like a bomb through that hedge.

By the time I raised my head, they were racing down the street. Jesse's legs were pumping so fast they were practically a blur. Fantasia was right behind him, *her* legs a blur, too.

Wow!

She was *fast!*

I watched as they disappeared around the corner. Then I worked my way out of the hedge and ran over to the blanket. Picking up the magazine, I stared at the cover. *Reel West.* Hey — Gertie had a subscription to that magazine. *Reel West* is for people who work in the movie business in Vancouver. It's full of pictures of actors. Gertie had explained that actors put their pictures in to advertise themselves to the people who make the movies.

What was Fantasia doing with *Reel West?* Unless … was this Gertie's copy? I leafed through it till I found the place where Fantasia had been writing. The page was full of photographs of actors, all smiling and looking glamorous.

Except for one. Right in the middle of the page, one actor was just a big black blotch. Fantasia had X-ed over the picture really hard with her black felt pen at least five or six times. You couldn't even tell who it was.

Unless you read the name underneath.

My breath stuck in my throat like a big furry ball.

Gertie Wiggins.

CHAPTER

10

THE FUZZY BALL GOT BIGGER. I SUCKED IN AIR —
hard. First Gertie's voice on the tape. Now
her face blacked out in a magazine?

Quickly I flipped through the rest of *Reel West*.
A few names were circled in pen, but they didn't
mean much — movie companies, maybe. I took a
quick peek into Fantasia's beach bag. Nothing
interesting there — just sun-tan lotion, a bottle of
nail polish and a package of gum. Nothing
suspicious in her potato-chip package, either,
except for a few extra-large extra-crispies. I
decided I'd better try one, just to make sure it
wasn't poisoned. It wasn't. Neither was the
second. Or the third.

When Jesse dragged himself into the courtyard
a few minutes later, I was waiting under the Big
Tree. Poor Jesse. His face was white as chalk and
his knees were so wobbly he had to lean against
the gate. He collapsed in a heap beside me.

"Jesse? You all right?"

"Uh."

"Did you get away?"

"Caught me." His chest was still heaving.

"Can I get you something? A glass of water?"

Eyes closed, he shook his head. Maybe if I said something cheerful …

"Oh well, at least she didn't catch both of us."

His eyes popped open. "She *screamed* at me, Stevie. Right into my face! For about five minutes! If you could die of screaming, I'd be dead right now. They'd be carrying me away on a stretcher."

I waited a minute and then said, "I looked through her magazine, Jesse. Want to know what I found?"

"NO!" Clamping his arms across his chest, he stared fiercely at the ground.

One thing I've learned about Jesse — sometimes it takes him a while to get over being upset. In the meantime, there's no point in even trying to talk to him. After a couple of minutes of ground-staring, he finally mumbled, "What?"

I told him about the blacked-out photograph of Gertie. "It was really weird. Fantasia scribbled those marks so hard they practically went through the page."

Jesse uncrossed his arms. "Why would she do that?"

I shook my head. Just one more question to add to the pile. No, not a pile — there was a Mount Everest of questions in this case. Before we could answer any of them, my dad came through the gate, a heavy-looking briefcase dragging in his hand. His shirt was damp and wrinkled.

"Dad! What are you doing home so early?"

"Too hot to think," he said. "How about you

guys? What have you been up to?"

I shrugged and gave him a Sappy Rabbits kind of grin. "Oh, you know ... stuff."

I felt Jesse tense beside me. He was staring past my dad.

Uh-oh. Fantasia was pushing her way backwards through the courtyard gate, loaded down with her bag, her Walkman, her soggy blanket and her empty potato-chip package. Her wet hair was plastered flat to her head. When she caught sight of me and Jesse, I thought for sure she was going to start screaming — the way she'd screamed in the laundry room, the way she'd screamed at Jesse. But all she did was stare. Jesse tucked both arms around his knees and scrunched down his head.

"I was thinking," said my dad. "This would be a great night to barbecue down at Locarno Beach. Maybe Jesse and his mom could come, too."

Fantasia was still standing there, her mouth a thin, tight line. Even though she was wearing sunglasses, I could tell that the eyes behind them matched her mouth — squeezed into skinny little slits.

"Sounds great," I said enthusiastically. "How about if Jesse and I make the salad? Why don't we go inside right this minute and and get started?"

"Well, uh, sure," said my dad. "Thanks, guys." He opened the door of our town house. Jesse shot through it so fast he nearly took my dad's arm off.

❖ ❖ ❖

I took the suspect list with me to Locarno Beach. Locarno is a long sandy beach, close to where we live, that faces out to the Pacific. Scattered around on it are huge drift logs — good for leaning against or tunnelling under. Behind it is a grassy park, full of giant old trees, where you can play ball or have picnics. After Kits Pool, Locarno Beach is probably my *second* favourite place in the world.

We had set up a blanket on the grass, and my mom and Jesse's mom were leaning against backrests on it, drinking lemonade and talking in slow, sleepy voices. The smell of smoky coals and sizzling meat made my mouth water as my dad cooked up burgers. Veggie-burgers for Jesse.

"What's in those things?" I asked when my dad passed him one.

"Nuts, grains, seeds — stuff like that. All ground up." Jesse took a big bite.

"And you like it?"

"Sure."

"Really?"

"Yeah. You know what I like best about it?"

"What?"

"It doesn't have any blood in it."

My dad passed me a plate. The middle of my burger was, uh, pink. Also a little ... well, runny. I squeezed.

Ewwwww ...

After dinner — mostly pasta salad for me — Jesse and I went for a swim in the ocean. The water was cool — ocean water always is around here — but with the setting sun glittering on its surface, it felt like we were like swimming in liquid gold. Above us, the sky was all swirly colours — pink, purple, orange, red. I could have floated on my back there forever.

The scream of a sea gull, swooping for a piece of garbage, broke the spell.

"Come on, Jesse. We've got work to do."

"Aw, Stevie … "

"Do you think that Tammy person is going to give up after one phone call? We could get rabbitted *tomorrow!*"

That got him. We huddled against one of the big logs, and I pulled out my suspect list. There was just enough light for Jesse to read it.

"Good work, Stevie. But it's missing a few things, isn't it?"

Ten minutes of concentrated thinking and writing later, the Suspect List looked like this:

GERTIE WIGGINS, MISSING PERSON
LIST OF SUSPECTS

1. TONCHIA BALASHNIKOFF — WANTS MOVIE ROLE
   — NASTY LUNCH TRICK!
2. FANTASIA BAYSWATER — VERY ANGRY! WHY?
   — MARKED-UP PHOTO

CLUES:
1. STOLEN NEWSPAPERS
2. WOMAN HIRED FROM PETS PLUS
3. PHONE CALL FROM GERTIE — CUT OFF

Jesse pointed at the first clue. "Shouldn't we be checking the newspapers? Maybe there's a clue in them. Some reason they got stolen."

I stared — at the list and then at him. "Jesse!

That's brilliant!"

"It is?"

I nodded. The first brilliant idea in days, and *Jesse* had had it. "I bet we can find copies in the co-op recycling bin."

"Tomorrow morning?" he said.

Grinning, we slapped hands.

"Tomorrow morning."

❖ ❖ ❖

Well, okay, so that was the plan. But if there's one thing I've learned about detecting, it's this — forget about plans. I came outside the next morning all set to search through the newspapers. Jesse's first words changed everything.

"Don't make any fast moves, Stevie. And don't stare. But look who's on Gertie's balcony."

Keeping my head low, I turned. A woman in a grey hat and beige shirt was moving from one hanging basket of flowers to another with a green plastic watering can.

"It's her," said Jesse. "The woman from Pets Plus."

Click, click, click in my brain and … "Perfect! We'll follow her."

Jesse's mouth dropped open. "Follow her! Where?"

"To her office — I hope."

"What for? She already told me that Pets Plus doesn't give out information about their customers."

"No problem," I said. In the movies, the detective always worms the information out somehow.

Sometimes there's a file, just sitting there on the edge of a desk, and the detective can sneak a look. Or else the detective zeroes in on the office snitch — the one person in the whole place who's ready to spill the story.

Jesse shook his head. "I can't go!"

"What? Another guitar lesson?"

"No! The Pets Plus woman has *seen* me, remember? She'll spot me right away."

"Oh," I said. Then, after a minute, "No she won't."

"Why not?"

I smiled. "You'll be wearing such a brilliant disguise," I told him, "even your own mother won't recognize you."

CHAPTER

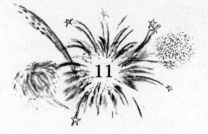

11

"*T*HIS IS A BRILLIANT DISGUISE? I LOOK LIKE A GOOF!"
Jesse was staring at himself in the hall mirror.
He was covered from neck to ankle by a black
trench coat I'd gotten at a co-op garage sale. Your
basic perfect detective coat, right? Just like you see
in the movies. I'd paid five dollars for it. So what
was his problem?

Maybe it was the hat. It was wide brimmed and
made out of yellow straw with a bright purple-
and-pink band. My aunt Lorna had brought back
from Mexico. Okay, so it wasn't the world's most
gorgeous hat. It covered his hair, didn't it?
Finishing off the disguise was a pair of aviator
sunglasses, the kind that shine like mirrors on the
outside. I'd found them in the junk drawer. Must
have belonged to some giant — they covered
most of Jesse's face.

Jesse pushed the hat to the back of his head.
He yanked it down on one side. He jerked it low
over one eye.

"Would you rather wear the toque?"

"In August?"

"Okay. Maybe not the toque."

"Maybe not the coat, either. What kind of idiot wears a trench coat in a heat wave?"

"Jesse, you look fine. The more of you that's covered up, the less there is for the Pets Plus woman to recognize."

Jesse pulled the hat brim down over his ears.

"Are you sure you don't want the wig?" It was bright, curly and orange — a leftover from Hallowe'en. I thought it made a fantastic finishing touch.

"NO!"

"Okay, forget the wig. Let's get going."

Two minutes later, we were crouched behind the hedge in the park. The Pets Plus woman would have to come out the front door of the apartment building. This was a perfect spot to spy from.

Jesse glanced around nervously. "What if Fantasia turns up again?"

"You're in disguise, remember?"

"You mean she won't recognize me?" For the first time that morning, he looked happy.

"Shh — look! There's the Pets Plus woman."

As she let herself out the front door, I got my first really good look at her. Jesse was right — she was about as ordinary as a person could be. Short brownish grey hair, a bit curly. Plain face you'd forget five minutes after you met her — small eyes, stubby nose, thin lips. Not tall, not short. Grey hat, beige shirt, beige skirt, brown purse and brown lace-up shoes. Across the pocket of her shirt were the words PETS PLUS.

And yet — was there something familiar about her? Maybe even something suspicious. In the movies, it's those ordinary, innocent-looking people you have to watch. I looked more closely.

Nah. She was about as suspicious as my grandmother. As she reached the corner of the street, Jesse and I slipped out onto the sidewalk.

"She's heading for the bus stop, Stevie. Quick! She'll get away."

A bus pulled up, and she got on, the door closing behind her. Jesse and I ran as hard as we could. I hammered on the door to make the driver wait for us. We slunk into the first empty seat. It had a newspaper on it, which I snatched up and held in front of our faces.

Jesse whispered, "I thought that when you're trailing someone, you're supposed to be incon … incon — you know."

"Inconspicuous?"

"Yeah," he muttered. "You're not supposed to stick out!"

I peeked over the top of the newspaper. The Pets Plus woman was about halfway back, staring out the window. Everyone else was staring at *us*. I shrunk back behind the paper.

"Where's this thing going, anyway?" asked Jesse.

"Downtown," I told him. "Keep your fingers crossed that she's heading to her office."

We drove over the bridge and along Granville Street, but she didn't budge. Past the movie theatres, past the big department stores and the downtown office buildings where most of the other passengers got off — and still she sat there. The bus reached the end of Granville and turned right. Finally, at Main Street, she stood up.

"Chinatown?" whispered Jesse.

We followed her off the bus into streets full of Chinese restaurants, stores, bakeries and butcher shops. The smells of fried noodles and something garlicky-gingery floated out of a restaurant, making my mouth water. The Pets Plus woman strolled along as if she had all the time in the world, peering in store windows at silk blouses, paper parasols, carved wooden figures. Jesse and I crept along behind her, staying close to the buildings and edging into doorways whenever we could — just like detectives in the movies.

"What's she doing?" Jesse was pressed up hard against a window. When he noticed what was on the other side, he yelped and leaped away. Barbecued ducks, reddish brown and dripping, hanging from giant meat hooks.

"She's sure not in a hurry," I said, watching as the Pets Plus woman checked out a set of wind chimes.

When she went into a store, Jesse and I followed. We backed right out again — the store was about as big as a bathroom, and she was the only customer.

"She's shopping, Stevie." Jesse's upper lip had little beads of sweat on it, and his face was getting red. "This is really dumb. If I'd wanted to follow a boring old person on her boring old shopping trip, I could have gone out with my *mother*. At least, *she* doesn't make me wear a coat."

I was about to answer when something caught my eye — or rather, my nose. I sniffed the air. "Do you smell anything?"

"Sure. Soya sauce, frying meat, spices — "

"Not those smells," I said. "Do you smell — ripe strawberries?"

Fantasia's perfume. I glanced around. The streets were so crowded it was hard to tell where the smell was coming from.

"There's a fruit store across the street, Stevie."

"Shhhh. She's coming out."

The Pets Plus woman's next stop was a little bakery café. Thank goodness. I was starved. She took a booth at the back, and Jesse and I slipped into one close to the door. We ordered warm Chinese buns — mine stuffed with barbecued pork and Jesse's with black beans. I don't know what the Pets Plus woman ordered. What I *do* know is how hard it was to follow her when she left.

In the movies, it always looks so easy. When the suspect gets up and leaves the restaurant, the detective just slaps some money down on the table and walks out, right? Well, that's the movies. In real life, you have to stand in line at the cashier while the people in front of you argue about their bill.

"Hurry!" squealed Jesse from the doorway. "She's getting away."

We had to run half a block to catch up — and then we almost banged into her. That's the other thing about tailing someone — deciding how close to get. Like, do you stay close enough to see what they're doing and risk being spotted? Or do you hang back and miss what they're doing and maybe even lose them? Believe me, it's not as easy as it looks.

"I'm sweltering," complained Jesse as we squished into a phone booth. "This coat is so hot you could bake bread in it."

I couldn't help feeling sorry for him. Jesse was the only person in Chinatown — probably in the whole city — wearing a coat.

"Undo the top button," I said. "Maybe — "

"Stevie, look! She dropped something."

The Pets Plus woman had pulled a camera out of her purse. A piece of white paper came with it and was drifting slowly to the pavement. A clue? We watched like hawks while she took pictures of a lamp post with a carved golden dragon on top. When she moved on, we ran over and snatched up the piece of paper.

"'Harry's Super Steam & Clean,'" I read. "'Let our professional dry-cleaning services take you from dirty to divine in just twenty-four hours!'"

"A dry-cleaning stub?" Jesse stuck his nose up against the paper. "We're following a stranger all over the city in a heat wave for a dry-cleaning stub?"

"So it's not a great clue." I shoved it in my pocket.

"It's not a clue at all, Stevie. Face it. This whole trip is a giant waste of time."

Well, okay. Following a poky old shopper around Chinatown, picking laundry stubs out of the gutter — this was *not* what you'd call a great day of detecting. Still … I didn't want to give up. Why not? All I can say is, it had something to do with my bones. I was beginning to think that that was where detective instinct is stored — in the bones. It's not what they teach you in science, of course. At school, they always say it's *marrow* in the bones. But it wasn't marrow that was telling me — as loud as if the message came through a microphone — to stay on the Pets Plus woman's trail.

Somehow I persuaded Jesse to stick with me — it probably helped that I didn't mention bones. He grumbled, but we followed the Pets Plus woman onto another bus, this one going to Stanley Park. For the next hour or two, we wandered around, watching her take pictures of squirrels and peacocks and Canada geese. We walked until our feet hurt. After the first hundred times or so, I had a pretty good idea of what Jesse would say when he opened his mouth.

"I can't *believe* I'm doing this!"

At four o'clock, she headed for the Sea Wall.

Jesse groaned. "Not the Sea Wall, Stevie!"

Stanley Park is a huge park, mostly woods. It's full of giant evergreen trees and almost surrounded by ocean. The Sea Wall is this walkway that takes you all around the outside of the park. You can walk it or Rollerblade or ride a bike.

"It must be eight kilometres around! You can't be serious."

He's right, said my head. No he's not, said my bones. What settled it was the memory of all those scenes I'd watched in mystery movies. Detectives slogging through dark alleys, wet tunnels, stinking swamps — dirty, tired, miserable, confused. Did movie detectives walk away from a tough trail? Never.

"Don't you want to see where she ends up?"

Jesse shook his head and sat down on a bench.

I cast around desperately for ideas. "Tonight is a fireworks night. If we hang around, we can see them up close. Please, Jesse?"

He grumbled, but after a minute he got up. I followed the Pets Plus woman, and Jesse followed me. The Stanley Park Sea Wall is about two sidewalks wide. On one side are the rocky cliffs and tall trees of the park. On the other side, it drops straight down to the shore. When the tide is in, ocean water laps up right against the wall. We joined the joggers, walkers and riders, trying to stay just the right distance behind the Pets Plus woman. Out in the harbour, sailboats skimmed past bigger fish boats and huge tankers. Gulls whirled and screeched, looking for dinner.

Speaking of dinner …

Luckily the Pets Plus woman stopped at a concession stand. Jesse and I kept one eye on her as we gulped down fries and called home from a phone booth. My worrywart parents weren't crazy about letting us stay for the fireworks, but when we promised to come home right afterwards, they finally agreed.

As I hung up the phone, I smelled it again — ripe strawberries. A Rollerblader with white-blond hair shot by and disappeared behind the concession stand. Could it be? Fantasia on Roller-blades? Hard to believe. But then, I never would have believed she could run, either ...

"Hey, Stevie, she's leaving."

One thing about that Pets Plus woman — she sure was a good walker. She charged along that walkway as if she'd just had a nap. Jesse and I shuffled along behind her, dragging our feet more with every step.

"I think I've figured it out," panted Jesse half a kilometre later. "She's training for the Olympics!" He stumbled, slowed, then walked over to the edge of the Sea Wall, where he plopped himself down. "That's it, Stevie. I've had it!"

The Pets Plus woman disappeared around a curve, still marching along as briskly as ever. Still as boring as ever, too.

I sighed and waited for a message from my bones. Awfully quiet in there. I hated to admit it, but it looked like Jesse had been right all along. My bones had led us on a wild-goose chase. A whole wasted day, and we didn't *have* days to waste. Maybe I should forget about being a detective. Maybe I should take up some other career — computer programming, maybe. Computer programmers get to sit down all day, right?

Collapsing beside Jesse, I yanked off my sneakers. My feet were all red and sweaty, and my toes were stuck together.

"Oooooooh," said Jesse, massaging his own feet. Below us, too far to reach, the sea was gloomy grey and fishy smelling.

"Look at that!" Jesse pointed into the air straight

in front of him. "Monster mosquito!"

It *was* pretty big, all right. Not big enough to fight with a jumbo jet, but big. For the next few minutes, Jesse and I traded lines from *Slap.* When we ran out of real lines, we made up our own.

"Dr. Stinger," said Jesse, "as the world's foremost mosquito, perhaps you can tell me something. Why do you think the human beings are suddenly behaving this way?"

"Well," I said, in a Dr. Kruger-type voice, "it turns out that we mosquitoes have made a terrible mistake about human beings. You see, for all these years, we have always believed they were stupid. The truth is — "

WHAM!

A hard shove. Right in the middle of my back.

The next thing I knew I was falling — down, down towards the murky, dark water. Jesse was falling beside me.

CHAPTER

12

WHOOSH! I SHOT THROUGH THE ICY-COLD surface like a bullet, gasping and sucking in huge mouthfuls of salty water. Down, down through the greeny black. Thrash, twist — sand? A somersault, a kick —

Which way was up?

Another flip, more gulps of salt water —

A hard kick — bursting up through the surface, choking, hacking — air!

Jesse! Where was Jesse? All I could see was his straw hat — floating on the surface.

"JESSEEEEE!"

A cough behind me.

He was still wearing the sunglasses. Water dripped down the mirrors. His arms, covered in big black coat sleeves, flapped up and down on the surface. He looked like a drowning bat.

"Who *did* that?" he choked out.

I looked up at the Sea Wall. No one.

We floundered around for a minute longer, hacking up more sea water. The cold raced through my cut-offs and T-shirt, going straight for my bones. I sucked in fishy air and coughed.

"We've got to get out of here."

"How?" asked Jesse.

Right. How?

The Sea Wall is exactly that — a wall. Straight down from the walk, straight up from the water. Have you ever tried climbing a wall? Especially a slimy, sea-slippery one?

Jesse gasped, his arms thrashing wildly. He looked like he was having trouble staying afloat.

"The coat!" I said. "It's weighing you down. Take it off!"

A few twists and grunts, and the black coat disappeared under the water.

Meanwhile, I was thinking hard. A mental picture, about ten minutes old, was pushing its way into my brain. "There's a stairway. Back around that last curve. We can swim to it."

"You sure?" I could hear fear in Jesse's voice.

"Yes," I said, trying to sound as if I meant it. This was no time to get in an argument, and anyhow, I was *almost* sure. At some places along the Sea Wall, there are stairways, so that when the tide's out, you can walk down onto the shore. I *thought* I'd seen one not far back.

"Follow me." Doing a sidestroke, I headed slowly back along the Sea Wall. I'd better be right. Jesse was already huffing and puffing behind me, splashing the water with each stroke. I looked up to the wall again. Maybe there'd be somebody who'd hear if we yelled for help?

Nothing but giant fir trees, blackish green, spiking the sky like knives. I searched the sea with my eyes. It had never looked so big before. I'd never felt so small …

Stay calm, Stevie.

"Do the backstroke for a while," I told Jesse — and myself, too. I flipped onto my back. The sky was even bigger than the ocean, getting darker every second, with the moon already a faint white shadow. After what felt like an hour, we finally rounded the curve. Treading water, we searched the wall with our eyes.

"It's not there, Stevie!"

I didn't answer. What could I say? We swam on like a couple of machines, but I knew we were ready to break down. Almost by accident, I reached out a toe and touched —

Sandy bottom.

"Jesse, we can stand up."

And over there — wasn't that a bumpy-looking bit on the wall? Yes — the stairway. We walked the last part, stumbling over small stones on the bottom, scraping ourselves on bigger rocks, sharp with barnacles and shells. By the time we reached the stairs, we were too tired to do anything but drag ourselves up and drop onto our stomachs.

"*She* did it, didn't she?" said Jesse finally. "The Pets Plus woman? She must have doubled back when we weren't looking."

Must have. After all, who else had been around? Who else knew where we were? Then I remembered.

"Ripe strawberries."

"What?"

"Fantasia's perfume. I've been smelling it all day."

Jesse sucked in his breath. "Are you sure?"

"I might have even seen her — back by the concession stand."

"You mean, Fantasia was following us?" Jesse's voice was hoarse. "All day? Ever since we left the co-op?" It was a creepy thought. Was it possible that while we were trailing the Pets Plus woman, Fantasia was trailing *us?*

Jesse shook his head, slowly, like he was still underwater. "I can't believe it, Stevie. Do you really think she'd try to drown us?"

"Well, somebody did." What if we hadn't been able to swim? What if we hadn't found a stairway?

"But … why?"

I shivered and rubbed my arms hard. "Remember that old movie we rented from Goldy's Oldies? *The Man Who Knew Too Much?* Well, that's us, Jesse. Ever since Gertie disappeared, we've been snooping around, asking questions, poking into other people's business. You and me — we're The Kids Who Know Too Much."

"What are you talking about? We don't know anything!"

"We know about a certain magazine," I reminded him, "with a certain killer X over a certain missing person's face."

"Ulp," said Jesse.

Something — a cool breeze? — tickled my back. I jerked around. If Fantasia really had been following us, maybe she was still there?

Jesse read my mind. "I'm outta here."

CHAPTER

13

A T LEAST SHE HADN'T STOLEN OUR SHOES. THEY were still where we'd left them. But my feet were such a mess — all scraped and swollen — I had to cram them in.

Getting home was *not* fun. Picture a couple of soggy, wiped-out kids stumbling through a crowd of happy summer fun seekers, and you'll get the idea. I'm sure the fireworks were terrific, but after what we'd been through, we wouldn't have noticed an earthquake. The good news was, we didn't smell any more strawberries.

It's at times like that that you really appreciate home. Your mom, your dad, your cat, a cosy spot in front of the TV, a tasty treat waiting in the kitchen ...

"Mom?" I called as I came in the door. "Dad?" There was a note on the kitchen table:

> Gone out for ice-cream sundaes.
> Back soon. There's cauliflower soup
> on the stove if you're hungry.
>   Love, Mom and Dad

Cauliflower soup? While *they* were eating sundaes? How could they do this to me — tonight of all nights? I stormed around the empty kitchen for a while, grumbling about the selfishness of grown-ups. Finally, I forced myself to check out the stove.

There it was — cold, white, practically solid, its surface all thick and gummy.

Maybe it would be okay if I heated it up.

Nope. Too tired.

But I was also really hungry. I stood there, staring at the soup. Tired ... hungry ... tired ... hungry ... tired ... hungry. Finally, I poked through the crust with a wooden spoon. Eeuugh. I picked up a lumpy spoonful. Eeuugggghhh ...

Okay, so I finished it. All except the crust. I was half starved, all right? I let out a huge burp. Perfect — all I needed yet was cauliflower burps. I was *definitely* going to check out computer programming.

Sometimes when my dad is tired, he says he's going to "crash." It's one of those old expressions from when he was a kid, meaning go to sleep. That night, I finally understood it. I could almost *hear* my body crash as it hit the mattress. My head was crashing, too, right into dreamland. Except — something was wrong. My feet were stiff.

I glanced down. They looked weird. They were poking straight up under the covers, like a couple of boards.

My feet! What had happened to my feet?

Swallowing a panicky scream, I whipped off the covers.

Oh.

Right.

It's okay, Stevie, I told myself. I bet *lots* of people forget to take their shoes off when they're really, really tired.

I untied my sneakers and threw them over the side of the bunk. That's when I heard it. Someone singing. Something about a lonely street and a heartbreak hotel.

Wait a minute. "Heartbreak Hotel" — that was an Elvis song. My dad sang it in the car sometimes.

Howard Biddlecombe? I stuck my head out the window. It was him all right. The twanging guitar and the toe-in-the-lawnmower voice were coming straight from his third-floor apartment.

Oh, man. I *really* needed to sleep.

I pulled my pillow over my ears, but it didn't help. After five minutes, I got out of bed and dragged myself up the stairs to our top balcony — the one that's off the study. It was right across the courtyard from Howard's apartment. I figured I might yell something clever at him. Like, Put a sock in it, Biddlecombe! Or, Keep it down, clown!

It would be better, of course, if Howard didn't know where the yell was coming from. Crawling across the dark study on my hands and knees, I carefully slid the glass door open. Then I crept out onto the balcony and crouched against the waist-high wall, inching up till my eyes poked over the top.

At first, I could hardly see him. He was standing behind a half-closed venetian blind, so all I could see was his shape moving back and forth. Oh, brother. Looked like he was imitating a rock star's movements — swaying and shaking. And his voice? If you listened long enough, it would make your teeth hurt. He was singing a different song now — about how he wanted somebody to be his *teddy bear!* I snorted. More screechy teddy bears. I let out a cackle. Before I knew it, I was in the middle of a giggling fit — choking, chortling, wheezing behind my hands. Tears ran down my face.

Then Howard stepped out where I could see him.

I stopped laughing.

Gertie's gold Elvis jacket!

Howard was wearing it! His face was bright red as he belted out a final moan.

It must have been the shock that made me stand straight up. Still, it would probably have been okay — no way Howard would ever have noticed me standing there in the dark.

Except …

"Stevie! What are you *doing?*"

The light flashing on behind me turned the study daylight bright and flooded onto the balcony. There I stood — lit up like the star of a Broadway show — staring straight into weird Howard Biddlecombe's apartment.

"Are you *spying* on the neighbours?" asked my dad.

Howard dropped his guitar and raced to the window. Venetian blinds rattled to the floor and snapped shut.

"Stevie, what's happened to you?" My mom pulled me into the study. "Your hair's all soaked and tangled, and your eyes — they're nearly closed. You look half dead." She turned to my dad. "Mike! Look at her. She looks half dead."

Half dead? I drooped my eyelids a little lower and waited.

"You get right to bed this instant." *That's* what I wanted to hear.

"And first thing tomorrow, young lady, it's Happy Rabbits!" That's *not* what I wanted to hear.

"Aw, Mom — "

"To bed, Stevie. Right now!"

Before I turned out the light, I took one last look across the courtyard. Howard's blinds were still closed. Except ...

I thought I saw a flicker of a blind. Then a dark spot. Yes. Howard had made a peek-hole in the blinds. He was in there, in the dark, staring out ... at *me*.

He knew that *I* knew that *he* had the jacket!

CHAPTER

14

I EXPECTED TO BE WOKEN UP BY WEIRD-HOWARD nightmares, but when I opened my eyes, sunshine was pouring through the window, and the voice singing in the courtyard was Tiffany's.

"One potato, two potatoes, three potatoes, five potatoes. Mashed potatoes, smashed potatoes, ten potatoes, thirty-eleven potatoes, hunnerd and nine potatoes — "

When she got to trillion potatoes, I couldn't take it any more. I got up and poked through the pile of clothes on the floor, hoping to find something halfway clean. Laundry, unfortunately, is another one of the chores my mom says I am old-enough-now-to-take-responsibility-for. Sifting through the dirty T-shirts, I wondered how detectives in movies get *their* laundry done. Maybe they don't bother. Lots of them are pretty rumpled-looking. I spotted my clothes from the day before, still lying where I'd stepped out of them. A bit damp, a little stiff. I pulled them on and went downstairs.

The kitchen was empty. I checked the clock.

Nine-twenty. The note on the table was in capital letters with underlining.

STEVIE:
WE TRIED TO WAKE YOU UP FOR
BREAKFAST, BUT YOU WERE TOO TIRED.
<u>WHAT ON EARTH WERE YOU DOING
YESTERDAY?</u>
I CALLED HAPPY RABBITS. THEY HAVE A
SPACE! <u>GO THERE TODAY</u> AND REGISTER!
I'VE LEFT A CHEQUE.

LOVE, MOM

P.S. TAMMY SAYS YOU CAN PICK UP YOUR
HAPPY RABBITS HAT TODAY, TOO.

There it was. In black and white. Sappy Rabbits had finally caught up with me.

The doorbell rang.

"Where have you *been*, Stevie? I've been waiting almost half an hour."

"Sit down," I told Jesse. "Eat some cereal. Have I got a story for you." As the two of us gulped down breakfast — my first, his second — I brought him up to date.

"The Elvis jacket!" Jesse's eyes lit up. "Stevie, it must be worth a fortune. Remember how excited Howard got when he saw it? And how he sang that song — 'you ain't never got a jacket and you ain't no friend of mine'?"

Ha! Finally he was admitting it — jacket, not rabbit.

I swallowed a mouthful of cereal. "One thing

I'm sure of, Jesse — there's no way Gertie would *give* Howard that jacket. And you know what else? I think he had a sunburn. I mean, it's hard to say because it was night-time. But I'm almost sure his skin was red."

"So?"

"So Howard *never* goes out in the sun."

"Who cares where he — " Jesse's eyes widened. "You mean, he might have got it in Chinatown yesterday? Or on the Sea Wall?"

An eerie picture was forming in my mind — Howard creeping along behind Fantasia, who was creeping along behind Jesse and me, who were creeping along behind the Pets Plus lady. Suddenly, I felt dizzy.

"I don't get it, Jesse. I mean, I *thought* I knew — with the strawberry perfume and all. But now, with the gold jacket — "

Jesse frowned and nodded. "I know what you mean. This case gets more confusing every second. Maybe we better take another look at the suspect list?"

I was getting up to look for it when I realized ... I already knew it off by heart.

"Hold on for a second, Jesse. Let me think."

I let my mind skip over the list. What had we missed? Suspects ... clues ...

Bingo!

"The newspapers!" I said. "The answer to this whole thing has *got* to be in those newspapers."

❖ ❖ ❖

"What exactly are we looking for, Stevie?"

We were sprawled out in the middle of my living room floor, newspapers spread all around us. It had taken a bit of digging, but we'd managed to find copies of all five missing papers in the recycling bin.

"Anything that might have a connection to Gertie." I picked up a thick entertainment section to start with. "I guess we'll know it when we see it."

But we didn't. We read articles about people fighting in far-off parts of the world. We read articles about forest fires in British Columbia. We read letters to Dear Abby and letters to the editor, book reviews and movie reviews, computer ads and fashion columns and weather reports. Jesse even read the comics.

"Checking *Garfield* for clues?" I asked.

"You never know."

At one-thirty we stopped for sandwiches.

"It's not looking good," said Jesse, munching on a cheese-and-avocado.

"We haven't looked at the classified ads yet."

"The classifieds! Stevie, that'll take forever."

He was right. The classified section was full of tiny little ads. People selling bicycles. People wanting pets. People renting apartments, looking for jobs, buying land, selling furniture, looking for antique trains — there were hundreds of them.

"This is hopeless," said Jesse. It was four-thirty, and we still hadn't found a thing.

"I know," I said, rubbing my eyes. "I'm going cross-eyed."

"Some of these ads are so dumb, too. Like, look at this one. 'Singles dance for people over fifty who love to polka.' What's a polka?"

"It's that dance where you hop up and down and whirl in circles as fast as you can."

Jesse grunted. "I bet it'll be a small crowd." He flicked a finger at the bottom of the page. "And look here. Someone's looking for a woman named Ramsbottom." He cackled and said the name again. "Ramsbottom! Can you believe it? I mean, what would the kids at school call you if you had a name like Ramsbottom?"

"Sheep Butt?" I suggested. "Lamb Bum?"

Jesse howled. "Lamb Bum! I love it! Lamb Bum! And wait till you hear the *rest* of her name. Listen to this. Agatha Gertrude Ramsbottom. Agatha! Gertrude! And then Lamb Bum! I don't *believe* it!"

I laughed, too. "Try it with the first names shortened. It's even worse. Aggie Gertie Lamb Bum!"

"Yeah!" snickered Jesse. "Aggie Gertie — "

He stopped. His eyes blinked. His mouth turned into a perfect round O.

I gasped. "That's it!"

"G-Gertie!" stammered Jesse.

"Short for Gertrude!" I said. "And Wiggins is her *married* name. Maybe her *single* name was Ramsbottom. Quick! Let me see that ad."

He handed me the paper, pointing at a little square. I read it out loud in a rat-a-tat burst:

Will Miss Agatha Gertrude
Ramsbottom, formerly of Leeds,

England, please contact Mr. Trevor
Throckington-Braithwaite at the
Pacific Grand Hotel on a matter of
urgency and importance. Contact
room 932 or leave a message with
the hotel by August 17.

"Look!" I squealed. "Leeds, England. Gertie's
from England!"

Jesse stabbed the paper with a finger. "And look
at the hotel!"

"The Pacific Grand! Of course! That's where I
met — I mean, was supposed to meet — Tonchia
for lunch. It can't just be a coincidence. Jesse,
this ad is the key to everything. I know it!"

Jesse squinted at it. "August 17. Stevie, that's
today!"

I looked at my watch; it was already four forty-
five. Picking up the phone, I started dialling.

"Pacific Grand Hotel," said the voice at the other
end.

"Could I speak to Mr. Throckington-Braithwaite
please?" I said. "In room 932?"

There was a pause. Then, "Just a moment,
please." Click.

A moment later, "Mr. Throckington-Braithwaite
has checked out."

"He what? But he can't — but when? Where did
he go?"

"I'm sorry, miss. I can't give out that information."

I thought fast. "But I'm his — his daughter!" I

said. "I'm only twelve years old. He was supposed to pick me up."

Jesse mouthed a WHAT??? beside me.

"Just a moment, please." Click. Another long pause, and then the voice returned. "Mr. Throckington-Braithwaite has gone to the airport. He left the hotel about ten minutes ago."

"Thank you, goodbye," I blurted and slammed down the phone.

I turned to Jesse. "Got any money?"

"Some, in my piggy bank. Why?"

"For a taxi. Let's go."

We raced over to Jesse's house. It was true. He actually had a piggy bank. It was round and pink and made out of china with a little curly tail.

"Don't you have a bank account?" I asked.

"Yes, I *do* have a bank account," said Jesse in a tense voice, "but I also happen to have a piggy bank that my grandmother gave to me on my fourth birthday. If I *didn't* have a piggy bank, we *couldn't* take a taxi, and if you make fun of my piggy bank, I am *not* going to give you any *money*. Got it?"

"Got it."

He emptied the piggy bank into my packsack while I called a taxi and scribbled a quick note for our parents. Ten minutes later, we were on our way to Vancouver International Airport.

CHAPTER

15

HUNDREDS OF PEOPLE, THOUSANDS OF PEOPLE, *millions* of people! Jesse and I stood just inside the airport doors, watching them. Business people in suits carrying briefcases, families with crying babies and huge piles of luggage, flight attendants, pilots, teenagers with huge backpacks. How were we ever going to find Mr. Throckington-Braithwaite?

In the movies, it always looks so easy. The detective rushes to the airport, makes straight for the airline counter, asks one or two quick questions and heads right for the mystery person — who is standing around, just waiting to be found.

But us? Even if we knew which flight Mr. Throckington-Braithwaite was taking, even if we knew which airline he was travelling on, we'd still have to wait in a huge line-up to even get to *talk* to an airline clerk.

"We'll never find him," moaned Jesse.

We were standing there, watching the rushing crowds and feeling hopeless, when we heard the intercom.

"Will Mr. Ashibito of Sato Electronics please come to the Canadian Airlines desk. Will Mr. Ashibito of Sato Electronics please come to the Canadian Airlines desk."

"That's it," I said. "We'll page him!"

"We'll what?"

"Get a message to him over the intercom," I explained. It took about twenty minutes, a bit of searching and some fast talking. Finally the intercom voice blared out our message.

"Will Mr. Trevor Throckington-Braithwaite please come to the Air Canada desk. Will Mr. Trevor Throckington-Braithwaite please come to the Air Canada desk."

"And now," I said, leaning against the Air Canada counter, "we wait."

After a minute, a skinny blond man in a green shirt and black pants came striding up to the counter. We looked at him hopefully. Nope. He was looking for his wife. Then came a big, heavy guy wearing a brown leather jacket, with an unlit cigar between his teeth. He seemed to be looking for someone.

"Trevor Throckington-Braithwaite?" I asked.

"Sam Flatburn," he muttered, chomping the cigar to the other side of his mouth.

After twenty-five minutes, we were almost ready to give up. "He must have already left," said Jesse. "We must have missed him."

"Excuse me," said a man's voice with an English accent. "I believe you're looking for me?"

We turned. The man was short, thin and bald,

except for a border of hair just around the bottom of his head. He had a skinny little moustache, crinkly blue eyes and glasses. His suit was navy blue with stripes, and he was carrying a briefcase.

"Trevor Throckington-Braithwaite," he said, holding out his hand. "And who might you be?"

"Stevie Diamond, short for Stephanie." I shook his hand. "And this is my friend, Jesse Kulniki. We're here about the ad in the paper. The one about Agatha Gertrude Ramsbottom."

At the word "Ramsbottom," a loud snort escaped from Jesse. Seeing me glare, he pulled his face into a serious expression. I'm sure I saw his lips forms the words "Lamb Bum."

"Ah," said Mr. Throckington-Braithwaite, "by all means." He glanced at his watch. "But we must be quick about it. I'm boarding in fifteen minutes."

I gulped. "We'll talk fast."

First I explained how we had this neighbour, Gertie Wiggins, who was missing, and how some people thought she was on holiday, only we knew there was something fishy going on. Then — I couldn't stop myself — I started babbling about the Elvis Forever Club and Howard's sunburn and Fantasia's magazine and the Pets Plus lady and even Tonchia's dog.

"And yesterday, Stevie and I got pushed off the Sea Wall," added Jesse. "We nearly drowned."

Mr. Throckington-Braithwaite looked a little confused. "I'm not sure I quite follow. Do you think this ... this Gertie Wiggins is the person I'm looking for?"

"Yes," I said. "I mean, we're not absolutely sure, but we know that Gertie is short for Gertrude and Wiggins is her married name, and — "

"And the hotel that Stevie was supposed to have lunch in — the Pacific Grand Hotel? — that's the same hotel *you* stayed in," said Jesse.

Mr. Throckington-Braithwaite's eyes crinkled even more, and the sides of his mouth curled up. I wasn't sure he believed us, but at least he seemed to think we were interesting.

"Jesse and I figured you must have some, uh, really important *reason* why you're looking for her?" I paused.

"Hint, hint," muttered Jesse.

Mr. Throckington-Braithwaite was silent for a moment. Then, "Perhaps if I tell you why I came to Vancouver, it will help us to get to the bottom of the matter."

Jesse and I both sighed with relief.

"I'm a solicitor," he said, putting his briefcase on the counter. "In London, England. Here in Canada you'd call me a lawyer. One of my clients — Cyril Ramsbottom — died recently. In his will, he left the bulk of his estate — his money, that is — to his niece, a woman named Agatha Gertrude Ramsbottom."

He paused.

"Uh-huh," I said. "So?"

"The problem is," said Mr. Throckington-Braithwaite, "no one in the family knows where Agatha Gertrude Ramsbottom might be. Apparently, she left England many years ago. The last anyone heard, she was living in Vancouver. I wrote a number of letters of inquiry, but nothing came of them. Finally, last week I flew over here and put some advertisements in the newspaper."

"Those are the ads we read," said Jesse.

"But I've had no response to my advertisements," said Mr. Throckington-Braithwaite, "except for, um, you two, of course." He raised his eyebrows. "And now I'm afraid I really must return to London." He tapped his watch.

"Wait!" I said. "We know who she is — this Agatha Gertrude Ramsbottom. And if you give us a chance, we'll … we'll figure out *where* she is, too."

Mr. Throckington-Braithwaite shook his head. "I'm afraid that won't do. You see, according to the terms of the will, I had to find Agatha Gertrude Ramsbottom within one year of my client's death. Otherwise, the estate goes to the next person in line. Two people actually — Agatha Gertrude's cousins, Cecily and Henry."

"One year? You have a whole year to find Agatha Gertrude?" Then I figured it out. "You mean, one year from the day Uncle Cyril *died!*"

He nodded. I was afraid to ask the next question. "So when did he die?"

"August 17," said Mr. Throckington-Braithwaite. "One year ago today."

Jesse gasped. "You mean if you don't find Agatha Gertrude *today,* these other relatives — Henry and whosis — get the money from the dead guy?"

"I'm afraid so," said Mr. Throckington-Braithwaite. He picked up his briefcase.

"But why are you leaving now?" I pointed at a

clock. "It's only 7:00 p.m. There are still five more hours in August 17."

He peered at me over the tops of his glasses. "My dear young lady! If Miss Ramsbottom hasn't turned up over the past year, surely you don't expect her to pop up here at the airport?"

"I — "

"This has all been most entertaining," he continued. "But you don't *really* expect me to miss my flight while you go searching for some mysterious woman whose location you do not even know and who probably has nothing whatsoever to do with my errand?"

"Well … yeah."

"Do you have any proof?" he asked. "Any actual physical proof of what you claim?

"Well … no."

Mr. Throckington-Braithwaite shook his head. "I'd better hurry, or I'll miss my flight."

Jesse and I skipped along beside him, double-time, as he rushed through the airport to the line-up of people waiting to go through the security gate.

This was it. Now or never.

"Please," I said. "If we can find her — Gertie — Agatha Gertrude — by midnight tonight, couldn't we let you know somehow? Wouldn't that be good enough?"

Jesse gaped. I knew what he was thinking. Find Gertie by midnight?

Mr. Throckington-Braithwaite sighed. "I'd need proof. A birth certificate, for example. I would have to receive it in London by midnight Vancouver time."

By midnight! How? But suddenly, I knew. When my mom and dad want to send something really quick, they fax it. I'm not sure how faxes work except that the message goes through the phone and makes a photocopy at the other end. If we could find Gertie, if she really did turn out to be Agatha Gertrude Ramsbottom, if we could find her birth certificate, if we could find a fax machine ...

If. If. If.

Mr. Throckington-Braithwaite set his briefcase down on the little belt that would take it through the security X-ray machine. A man and a woman in uniform were holding those metal detector things they run over people's bodies before they get on airplanes. A sign said, Passengers Only Beyond This Point. In five seconds, he'd be gone.

"We'll fax it to you," I said.

He turned and smiled. "Jolly good idea," he said. "Why don't you do that?" It was obvious from the way he said it that he didn't believe for one second we were ever going to send him a fax. It was even *more* obvious that he didn't believe Gertie was Agatha Gertrude.

And why should he? Where was the proof?

"It's been a pleasure meeting you both," he said. "Good luck with your search for Mrs., um, Wiggins, was it?" He reached out a hand and shook both of ours again.

"Goodbye," he said and turned to go through the security gate.

"Wait!" I said. "Where do we send the fax?"

He stopped, smiled and handed me a business card.

"Oh," I said. "I have business cards, too. But I, uh, don't have one on me."

Mr. Throckington-Braithwaite chuckled. "That's all right," he said. "You might just fax *that* to me, as well."

We watched him step through the gate and walk down the long passageway that led to the planes. After he had disappeared around a corner, Jesse turned to me.

"Fax Gertie's birth certificate to London? Stevie, what are you talking about? We don't have the faintest idea where she is."

"No," I agreed. My mind was racing now — zapping from idea to idea to idea so fast I could hardly breathe. "But I think I know how to find her."

"You do? How?"

"By taxi."

"Another taxi? Where are we going now?"

I pulled him towards the airport doors.

"To pick up some laundry."

CHAPTER

16

THE TAXI DROPPED US OFF IN FRONT OF HARRY'S Super Steam & Clean Dry-Cleaning. Good — it was still open.

I felt in my pocket for the dry-cleaning stub that had dropped out of the Pets Plus lady's purse. If my plan worked, we could use it to pick up whatever clothes had been left here for dry-cleaning. And if we were really lucky, the clothes would have an address on them.

"Act like you know what you're doing," I muttered to Jesse.

"I *don't* know what I'm doing."

"Me neither. Fake it."

As we stepped inside, I tried hard to look twenty instead of twelve. The man behind the counter, a grey-haired guy with a beard — Harry, maybe? — glanced up.

"Can I help you?"

"I've got some, uh, dry-cleaning to, uh, pick up," I said in a deep, twentyish voice.

Too deep, I guess. "Pardon?" said Harry.

"Dry-cleaning. Here!" I shoved the stub across the counter.

Was it my imagination, or did he give me a suspicious look? Did he know that the clothes weren't mine? That I'd never in my whole life been inside this store before? He took the stub and checked through the racks of clothes that were moving in slow circles behind him, hanging on wire hangers and wrapped in clear plastic.

He brought us three hangers. Two held pants, and the third held a dress.

"Thanks," I said, taking the hangers from him. Giving Jesse a nod, I turned to go.

"Hold on a minute," said Harry.

We stopped.

"That'll be $10.98."

"Ouch!" said Jesse.

I gave Harry a weak smile. "You mean we didn't pay you when we brought this stuff in?"

Now Harry was definitely looking suspicious. I reached into my packsack. Paying Harry left us with thirty-seven cents.

Outside, I grabbed the tag attached to the hangers. "Is there an address?" I asked, shoving it at Jesse. "I can't look."

Taking the clothes, he peered at the tag. "We've got it, Stevie! It's 1196 Harlen Street."

I knew where that was — only about ten blocks away. We set off at a slow run. As we started to get closer, I felt a butterfly flip-flop in my stomach. What if I was wrong? Even worse — what if I was *right?*

Five or six butterflies later, we were standing in

front of a small wooden gate with the number 1196 on it. The gate was in the middle of a gigantic hedge — probably twice as tall as me and Jesse. It surrounded the whole yard, except for where the gate was. I peeked into the yard.

A tall thin old house — faded grey with dark red trim — sat at the back of the lot. It had a small, sagging porch with a couple of wooden lawn chairs on it. Thick bushes full of big yellow roses were scattered across a scruffy-looking yard.

Jesse poked his head over the gate. "No lights on," he said. Good point. It wasn't really dark yet, but it *was* dark enough to turn on lights.

Just as if we'd ordered it, a bright light appeared in the biggest of the front windows. The curtains were pale, and we could see a couple of people behind them, moving their arms as if they were talking.

"We have to get closer," I said.

"It's not dark enough, Stevie." Jesse's voice was getting that I'm-not-sure-I-want-to-do-this sound.

"Time's running out," I said. "If we run from bush to bush, we should be okay." Putting my hand on the gate handle, I pushed … slowly, slowly …

Creeeeeeeeeeeeeeeeeeeek!

"Shhhhhh!" Jesse darted back behind the hedge.

"Well, geez. Why doesn't somebody oil this thing?"

Almost on my hands and knees, I crept through the gate and darted to the first bush. Squatting behind it, I pressed myself up against the prickly branches.

"Stevie! Wait for me!"

"Ssshhhh!"

More squeaking, then a heavy thud behind me as the gate closed. Skitter, skitter across the grass, and Jesse was beside me.

"Is this close enough?" he asked. "Can you hear?"

"No." I pointed. "That bush next!"

I started to move, then stopped. "Uh, Jesse?"

"Yeah?"

"Lose the laundry."

"Huh?"

I pointed at his hand, which was still clutching the dry-cleaning hangers. The plastic-covered clothes were dragging in the grass.

"Oh. Right." He looked around, then hung them neatly on a branch.

I sighed.

"Well, what am I *supposed* to do?" he asked. "Eat them?"

I snatched the clothes and jammed them in among some leafy, lower branches. Then I took off across the lawn again, with Jesse right behind. Two bushes later, we were almost at the porch.

Jesse was breathing heavily now, chewing on his lower lip. "I think this is close enough, Stevie. I think if we try really hard, we can hear every single word they say. I mean, I don't think it's a good idea to go up there — on the porch, I mean — because if somebody comes out — "

"The only thing I can hear is *you*, Jesse."

"Okay. I get it. I'll keep quiet. Fine."

There were two voices, a man's and a woman's.

They seemed to be arguing, but I couldn't make out what they were saying.

"I'm going up on the porch."

"But, Stevie — "

I waited till I heard voices again, then dashed across the last stretch of grass — onto the walkway, up the wooden stairs two at a time, and into the corner of the porch, right behind the door.

Safe! I hadn't made a sound.

Looking back, I saw Jesse peeking around the bush. His eyes were enormous, but he was hunched over, ready to follow. I put a finger over my mouth, signalling him to be quiet. He nodded to show he understood.

He *was* quiet, too.

It was that loose bottom step that *wasn't*. When Jesse put his foot on one side of it, the other side shot up. When his foot came off, the lifted end dropped with BANG as loud as a firecracker.

If we'd been movie detectives, we would have raced for our getaway car. We would have peeled away in a squeal of tires, a cloud of gravel and a hail of flying bullets.

But Jesse and me? What *we* did was leap at each other, screeching and clutching hands. Not for long — but long enough for a big red-headed guy to charge through the door and grab us. Before you could say Sherlock Holmes, we were dragged inside the house and dumped in front of a grouchy-looking woman with brownish grey hair.

The Pets Plus woman.

I was right!

Not that it did me much good.

"Are these the two you were talking about?" asked the big guy. He had an English accent. Right again. He also had thick muscular arms, hands as big as baseball gloves and the same nose as the Pets Plus woman. It looked a lot like a —

Potato!

Just like Gertie's! All three of them — Gertie, the Pets Plus woman and the big guy — they *all* had potato noses. That's when I knew for sure my theory was right. The Pets Plus woman was Cecily Ramsbottom, and the big guy was Henry. They were Gertie's creepy cousins from England.

"That's them," said Cecily. "Pushy little blighters."

"You said you'd got rid of them yesterday in Stanley Park."

"Yes, but they're a pair of leeches, they are." She grabbed my cheek between her thumb and finger and squeezed. "They — just — don't — let — go!" With each word, she yanked at my cheek.

"Ow! *You* let go!" I yelled. "Potato nose!"

From the way her teeth clenched together, you could tell she'd been called that before. And she *didn't* like it.

"Into the cellar!" snarled Cecily, staring down her nose at me. She turned and headed into a dark hallway. Henry's big ham hands half-dragged, half-pushed us after her. At the end was a door. The cellar? Cobwebs? Spiders? Rats?

The next thing I knew, we were tumbling down

a narrow flight of stairs. The door slammed behind us, and I heard the rapid click of the lock.

"Acchh — the children!" a familiar voice sang out.

I turned.

Tonchia! She was sitting at a little round table, holding a cup of tea. Across from Tonchia, her mouth hanging open in astonishment, sat Gertie. The two of them couldn't have looked more surprised if a couple of Martians had dropped through the ceiling.

CHAPTER

17

"STEVIE! JESSE — " GERTIE ROSE SLOWLY TO HER feet, hands gripping her chair, as we staggered down the last few steps.

For the next minute or two, we didn't say anything. Too busy hugging. I never knew till that second how much I'd missed Gertie — her lopsided grin, her rough-as-nails voice, even her stubby potato nose. Not to mention her hugs — Gertie gives awfully good hugs. Tonchia got in the act, too, kissing our cheeks and showering our backs with quick little pats.

"Such clever children," she kept saying. "It is like a miracle, no? You have found us." I grinned, but a little voice in my head asked, so what? Now we were *all* trapped.

Not a cosy trap, either. We were in a rough, ugly basement with walls of solid concrete — except for a few dark, skinny windows up high, a door in one corner — and the one at the top of the stairs, of course. Tall cupboards and shelves leaned against two of the walls, and the floor was dull grey tiles. The only light in the whole place came from a bare bulb hanging from the ceiling. The table where Tonchia and Gertie had been sitting held a teapot, two cups and a deck of scattered cards. There were also some wooden chairs and a couple of raggedy old couches — one checked and one flowered — facing each other across a dirty brown hooked rug.

"What are you two *doing* here?" Gertie finally asked after about the twentieth hug.

"We're rescuing you!" Jesse blurted. As soon as the words were out, his face fell. He must have noticed how completely unrescued Gertie and Tonchia were.

"What happened to *you,* Gertie?" I asked. "Everyone thinks you've gone on vacation."

"Vacation!" Gertie stiffened. "With a big audition coming up? With two children in my care? Vacation, my eye. I was snatched!"

"Snatched?"

"Snatched like a purse!" She reached out a hand and grabbed at the air. "That hot afternoon after our last rehearsal. Remember I said I was going out for a newspaper? Well, there I was, at the newspaper machine, looking through my change. And suddenly, out of nowhere come those two awful people upstairs! 'Come on, Granny,' they say, 'it's time to go home.'"

Gertie huffed with annoyance. "As if I was anybody's blooming granny! The next thing, I'm being hauled into the back seat of a car by that great bonehead of a man. At first, I thought maybe they'd mistaken me for their *real* granny. But oh no, it was me they wanted, all right. Although what they want with me, I still can't figure out."

Tonchia was fluttering her hands with excitement. "I, too, was snatched," she said.

"How?" asked Jesse. "When?"

"You remember when you children so nicely visited me? You told me about stolen newspapers, yes?" Tonchia's voice was quick and breathless. "Well, the next morning, I am reading my newspaper very carefully like a — how do you say? — private eyeball — "

"Private eye," interrupted Jesse.

"Yes, yes — and what do I see?"

"What?"

"Gertie's name. Her name from the old days before she got married. Somebody is wanting to talk to her at the Pacific Grand Hotel. Who could this be, I ask myself. I must go to see this Mr. Throckington-Braithwaite."

Tonchia's dark eyes darted around, bright and lively. "So I phone you. I say come, Stevie, Jesse, meet me at the Pacific Grand Hotel. And I get in a taxi, so excited. It is like a great mystery, no? The taxi goes very fast — whiz, whiz. I arrive at the hotel early. Aha, I think — maybe I can find out the answer *before* the children come. Maybe I can surprise them! So I go to the hotel desk and I ask for Mr. Throckington-Braithwaite. The hotel desk clerk, he is phoning to Mr. Throckington-Braithwaite's room. But then suddenly another man is standing there — a large red-haired man."

"The lunkhead upstairs," muttered Gertie.

"Yes — him," said Tonchia. "He tells me that *he* is Mr. Throckington-Braithwaite."

I shook my head. "Jesse and I *met* Mr. Throckington-Braithwaite. He's little and bald."

Tonchia raised her arms into a shrug. "Well, how I am to I know this? He tells me to come outside to talk. And bing, bing, just like that" — Tonchia snapped her fingers — "he pushes me into a car, and we are driving, driving, fast across the city. He brings me here — to this dark little room under this big old house. It is terrible, yes? But it is also good, because here at last I find my dear friend Gertie." She reached for Gertie's hand.

"What a good friend you are, Tonchia," said Gertie, squeezing the hand. Then she took my hand, and Tonchia reached for Jesse's. The next thing you know, we were all four holding hands, our eyes filled with tears. Yeah, yeah, I know it's corny, but that's what happened.

"Enough of this blubbering," Gertie said finally, pulling a tissue out of her pocket and blowing her nose. "Tonchia and I know how *we* got here. What we want to know is, how did you kids get here?"

So Jesse and I told the whole story — how we'd followed the Pets Plus woman all over Vancouver and how we'd found the dry-cleaning stub that had led us to this house. We told about getting pushed off the Stanley Park Sea Wall, too, but maybe that was a mistake. Gertie looked horrified.

"*She* pushed you? The woman upstairs?"

"We weren't sure at the time," I said. "But the big guy just admitted it."

"She must have doubled back and snuck up

behind us when we weren't looking," said Jesse.

"But you might have been drowned!" cried Gertie. "You might have been swept out to sea!" Grown-ups, I notice, like to do this — think of all the awful things that *could* have happened, even when none of them did.

"But *why* did she push you?" asked Tonchia. "Who *are* those wicked people?"

"I'm getting to that," I said. With Jesse helping, I raced through the rest of the story — spotting the newspaper ad, Mr. Throckington-Braithwaite, the airport, the money in the will. Maybe I said it all too fast. At the end, Gertie and Tonchia looked more confused than ever.

"It's simple," said Jesse. "Are you Agatha Gertrude Sheep Butt?"

Gertie and Tonchia stared. Realizing what he'd said, Jesse turned bright red. "I mean, er, are you Agatha Gertrude Ramsbottom?"

"Well, I used to be," said Gertie slowly. "Before I got married."

"Then Mr. Throckington-Braithwaite came to Vancouver to find you," I said. "He wanted to tell you that your uncle Cyril left you money in his will."

"Money?" Gertie's forehead wrinkled up. "Uncle Cyril? All he ever had was a little fish-and-chip shop down at Brighton."

"Well, he must have made some money somehow," I said, "or people wouldn't be going to all this trouble."

Tonchia stamped her foot. "Sheep? Fish? I do

not understand. Who *are* those people upstairs?"

"Don't you see?" I said. "They're Gertie's cousins! Cecily and Henry Ramsbottom! "

Gertie's mouth dropped open. "Cousin Cecily? Cousin Henry? Why, they were just babies the last time I saw them."

"Rotten little babies, I bet," muttered Jesse. "Grew up into rotten big adults."

"They even *look* like you," I told Gertie. "Cecily has your po — I mean, your nose."

Tonchia gasped. "Yes, of course! It is true, Gertie. This Cecily looks very much like you used to look — back in our days in Hollywood." I remembered the photograph of Gertie in Tonchia's apartment. No wonder the Pets Plus woman had looked familiar.

"Nonsense!" Gertie tossed her orange-and-grey hair. "I don't look a bit like that dreadful woman." She searched our faces. "Do I?"

One by one, we all nodded.

"Oh, dear," said Gertie.

"Your rotten old cousins are after Uncle Cyril's money," said Jesse. "They've been trying to keep you and Mr. Throckington-Braithwaite apart so you won't get your inheritance. That's why they stole your newspapers — so you wouldn't see the ads."

"And when they saw you trying to *buy* a newspaper," I added, "they must have gotten desperate."

"They told me I was their guest." Gertie sounded amazed. "I suppose they thought I'm

some dotty old woman who'd believe anything —
that they could just keep me here and I'd never
figure anything out."

"But why did they kidnap *me?*" asked Tonchia.

"Henry must have been watching the hotel," I
told her, "to see if anyone showed up with
information for Mr. Throckington-Braithwaite.
When *you* turned up, he grabbed you before you
could talk."

Gertie clucked her tongue. "The devils!"

"Cecily's been going in and out of your
apartment all week, Gertie," added Jesse. "She's
been telling everyone she works for a company
called Pets Plus. She even has a shirt that says Pets
Plus." He frowned. "How'd she *get* that shirt?"

Gertie grunted. "Any idiot can embroider a few
letters on a shirt."

Embroider?

"Uh, not exactly *any* idiot," I said.

Jesse still looked puzzled. "How did she get
into Gertie's apartment?"

"With my keys, of course!" said Gertie. "They
took my purse. All my keys were inside." She
slapped her hand hard on the table. "Oh, they *are*
rotten — to the core!"

Tonchia shook an angry fist at the ceiling.
"Swine!" she yelled. "Cockroaches! Maggots!"

"Shhhh," I warned. "Better keep it down. We
don't want Cecily and Henry to know we're on to
them."

"Yes, of course." Gertie's voice dropped to a
murmur. "Our only hope is for them to think we

don't know a thing." Tonchia nodded, and Jesse drew a line across his lips with one finger.

"Bit late for *that,*" said a voice from the stairs.

Cecily. Staring down from the top step. How had I ever thought she looked ordinary? That woman had the meanest eyes I've ever seen — nasty, little piggy eyes. Her nose was piggy, too, when you saw it from this angle, and her skin was pale and pasty — dough before it's baked.

How long had she been standing in that doorway? How much had she heard?

"Clever of you to have worked it all out," she snapped. Slowly, the door closed. Click. Then click again.

Everything. She'd heard everything.

18

TONCHIA WHIMPERED SOMETHING IN A FOREIGN language.

"What an idiot I am!" said Gertie. "Blabbering on, not even thinking — "

"No, no." Tonchia shook her head. "It is me. I have such a very large mouth, you see. I spoke stupidly, foolishly."

"We're dead meat," moaned Jesse. "We're toast!" Slumping forward, he buried his face in his arms.

Tonchia nodded, looking worried. "We are toasted meats."

I waited for Gertie to say something encouraging. I wanted her to tell us to snap out of it and for-goodness-sake-get-a-bit-of-backbone — to scold us into action, the way she had scolded Howard Biddlecombe. But I guess she'd been locked up too long. Taking off her glasses, she covered her face with her hands.

There was only one thing to do.

"For crying out loud, Jesse, get a grip. All of you — get a grip!" I glanced at my watch. "It is now 9:58 p.m. We have exactly two hours, one minute and thirteen seconds to escape from this basement, get Gertie's birth certificate and fax Mr. Throckington-Braithwaite in London."

That did it. They all sat up straight.

"Have you gone completely *nuts?*" asked Jesse.

"We have been here for days now," said Tonchia. "Gertie and I, we have looked everywhere for a way out. We have searched every — how do you say? — crook and nanny?"

"Nook and cranny," I said. "There's *got* to be a way out. And you know what they say — four heads are better than two."

"*Who* says that?" asked Jesse. "I never heard anybody say that."

"The point is, if we all work together, we can do it. I know we can."

Before he could answer, Gertie held up a hand. "Stevie's right. Yes, Tonchia, I know, we've gone through this place with a fine-tooth comb. But we have to make an effort. At least we'll go down trying."

Go down trying? That wasn't exactly what I had in mind. Still, it was good to have Gertie on my side. Well, sort of …

"Let's start with the doors," I said, pointing to the one in the wall. "What's that?"

"A bathroom," said Gertie. "Forget it. There's no way out of there."

"Any chance of getting out that way?" I pointed to the door at the top of the stairs.

She shook her head. "They keep it locked. Except when they bring us food. Once they forgot, and I got as far as the phone — but they caught me." So I'd been right about that phone message from Gertie.

"Windows?" I glanced at the small black squares high up in two of the walls.

Tonchia shrugged sadly. "Two days ago, Gertie and I — we climbed on the chairs. We thought maybe we could push open the windows. But there are heavy shutters on the outside, holding them shut. They must be nailed down."

No windows, I thought. And no doors. You'd have to be Houdini to get out of this place. Maybe Jesse was right. Maybe we should just give up and —

Jesse snapped his fingers. "I've got it! What if we lured them down here? I could fake an asthma attack and — "

"And what?"

"Super Glue! We could put it on the stairs. When Cecily and Henry run downstairs, their shoes would get stuck. They'd be trapped!"

Gertie shook her head. "Number one, they probably won't care if you have an asthma attack."

"Number two," said Tonchia, "they can just take their shoes off, no?"

"Number three," I said. "Do you *have* any Super Glue?"

Jesse fell back into his slump. "Toast!"

Gertie suggested throwing pepper in Cecily's and Henry's faces. Unfortunately, we didn't have any pepper.

Tonchia thought of knocking Cecily and Henry out by putting sleeping pills in their wine. She said she saw it in a movie.

"No sleeping pills," said Gertie.

"No wine, either," I added.

Like I said, real detecting just isn't like the movies. But talking about the movies got me thinking — about the lock on the door. Movie detectives can pick a lock faster than most people can pick their noses.

"Anybody got a hairpin?" I asked. "Or a nail file?"

Gertie had a hairpin, and Tonchia found a nail file in her purse.

"I'll try the lock," I said. "In the meantime, you guys check the rest of this place — floors, walls, ceilings, the works."

I climbed the steps and stared at the door. How the heck do you pick a lock? It's not exactly something they teach you in school. Do you just stick something in the keyhole and wiggle it around, or what?

I tried the hairpin first. Wiggle, poke, twist, wiggle some more. In seconds, the hairpin was a bent, mangled wreck. The nail file lasted about a minute before it broke in half, leaving the pointed end stuck in the keyhole. As I was jiggling it loose, I heard voices on the other side. Cecily and Henry were arguing.

"I *told* you to stay around here," he complained. "I told you it wasn't safe to wander about, attracting attention. But no, you had to keep going back to her apartment."

"I had to convince those nosy neighbours that the old dear was off on holiday, didn't I?" said Cecily.

"Yes, well, it wasn't just the apartment. You've spent the whole last week gadding about Vancouver like a tourist."

"Why shouldn't I be a tourist?" said Cecily. "I've come all the way from London, haven't I? Did you expect me to sit like a lump in this dreary old house you rented? Might as well take a look round the city while I'm here. No harm done."

"No harm?" snapped Henry. "Those bleeding kids followed you back here. They know everything! If we let them go, they'll run straight to the police."

The next bit was muffled. Then I heard Henry's voice again. " ... never intended to capture ... never intended to kidnap anyone! You said it would be simple. You said we'd never get caught. You said — "

"Oh, Henry, stop whining," said Cecily. "We'll deal with them in the morning."

"Deal with them?" said Henry. "And how exactly do you reckon we'll *deal* with them?"

Yes, I thought — how? Cecily's answer was muffled. I pressed my ear against the door so hard it hurt, but all I got was a mumble.

"Cecily!" Henry burst out. "You can't really mean — "

This time, Cecily's voice was as crisp and clear as ice. "Don't you go all soft on me, Henry Ramsbottom. I certainly don't intend to spend the rest of *my* life in jail."

CHAPTER

19

"STEVIE?" GERTIE'S VOICE WHISPERED UP FROM THE bottom of the stairs.

Should I tell them what I'd heard? No. Not unless I had to. Jesse was nervous enough already.

"No luck," I said, trudging downstairs.

Jesse was huddled on the couch, looking mopey. "Forget it, Stevie. It's hopeless. We've gone over every inch of this place — doors, windows, floor, even the ceiling."

"Not *every* inch," I said, looking around. "Has anyone checked behind those?" I pointed at the tall cabinets and shelves that stood high against the wall.

Tonchia shook her head. "They are very heavy, Stevie."

I nodded. "Then we'd better get started."

At first, it seemed impossible. Two old women and two twelve-year-old kids are not exactly your ideal moving crew. But it's funny — put a bunch of people's strength together, and it somehow ends up being more than you expect. It's like adding up one and one and one and one and getting ten. Nearly killed us, but in the end, we managed to move a tall wooden wardrobe, a set of high shelves and a huge old dilapidated cabinet.

That's where we found it. Behind the cabinet. It wasn't much, but you could spot it if you looked closely — a small square of wood, painted over a long time ago. A faint crack line all around its edges was the main clue.

"What is it?" asked Jesse.

"I don't know. Looks like a little old door." I began to chip away at the dried paint with the broken nail file. Poky, slow work, especially with three people breathing in my ears. Gertie found a spoon and started chipping, too. Finally, most of the dried paint was picked out of the cracks.

"Okay," I said. "Here goes." Shoving the nail file into a side crack, I tried to pry it open. It didn't move.

Gertie shoved her spoon into the crack on the other side and the two of us pried together. Jesse found an old curtain rod and joined in at the top. At first, nothing. Then I felt it — the little wooden panel shifted slightly.

"It's working!" cried Jesse. "It *is* a door. It's opening."

Another tug and the panel pulled away in my hands, leaving a square-shaped opening in the wall. I stuck my head in — right through a cobweb.

"Ugghh!" Pulling back, I swiped at my face. Hair, too. Then I stuck my head in again. No way a measly spider web was going to stop me now.

"What is it?" asked Jesse. "A secret passage?"

"No." I felt like crying. "Just a closet — with ropes up the side."

"Ropes?" said Gertie. "Here, let me take a look."

She stuck her head inside. When she pulled it out, her face was one huge grin. "It's a dumb waiter."

"A waiter? In there?" Jesse's eyes bugged out. "How do you know he's stupid?"

"Not that kind of waiter," said Gertie, laughing. "A dumb waiter is like a little elevator. You pull it up and down with ropes in the sides. They used to put dumb waiters in houses in the old days to move things from one floor to another. We had one in the house where I grew up. Mother used it to move the laundry up and down from the basement."

I hardly dared ask. "Does it still work?"

"I don't know. Those ropes look pretty frayed. Try pulling on them."

I crossed all my fingers for a second, then grabbed hold of the rope and pulled. There was a creaking sound — wood against wood — and slowly, in a shower of dust, the ceiling of the closet began to come down. Gertie was right! It *wasn't* a ceiling! The thing that was coming down to our level was an elevator platform.

Getting it all the way down was slow, dirty and noisy. Too noisy, with plenty of creaking and groaning. Nothing we could do except hope Cecily and Henry couldn't hear it upstairs. When the platform finally reached bottom, I peered inside again. A tall shaft rose up into total blackness. If

Gertie was right, there must be a door on another floor.

I took a deep breath. "How much weight can this thing hold?"

Gertie shook her head. "I know what you're thinking, Stevie, but it was only meant for dishes and laundry."

"How about just one person?" I said. "One small, light person?"

"It must!" Tonchia clapped her hands together. "It must lift one of us to go for the police."

Gertie thought for a moment, then nodded.

"Who's the lightest?" I asked. It was like a party game. The winner of the Lightest-Prisoner-in-the-Basement Contest turned out to be Tonchia.

She looked alarmed. "Stevie, it is not possible. My body — it will never bend that way."

I glanced at the small square in the wall. Tonchia was right. You'd have to practically pretzel yourself to squeeze in there.

I looked at Jesse. "I guess you're it." I was ten pounds heavier than he was, and Gertie was heaviest of all.

"Me?" squeaked Jesse. "Go up there? In that? By myself? No way."

He looked at Gertie for help, then at Tonchia, then at me. Nobody said a word.

"I have claustrophobia," he said. "I panic in a closed-in place. I also have this horrible fear of the dark."

He waited.

"Spiders, too."

Nobody answered.

"And heights! Did I ever tell you about the time I was on a Ferris wheel and threw up on the people underneath? Man, it was gross. It was — "

He stopped. I'm still not sure exactly what happened, but it might have had something to do with the looks on Tonchia's and Gertie's faces. There was a long, heavy silence.

"Okay," said Jesse. "I'll do it."

Seconds later, he had squished in through the little opening and was perched on the tiny platform.

"Knock once on the platform if you want us to pull you higher, twice if you want us to stop," said Gertie. "The next door will probably open into a kitchen. Try to find your way out of the house and call the police."

"Good luck, Jesse." Tonchia leaned into the opening and kissed him on the cheek. From the expression on her face, you'd have sworn he was going off to war.

Jesse looked like he was going to throw up. He nodded, white-faced, and gave a thumbs-up signal. He even tried to smile, but his mouth was wobbling too hard. Gertie and I pulled on the rope. A loud squawk, and the platform began to rise. More creaks and groans. Jesse's head disappeared, then his shoulders, his waist and then the platform rose out of sight. He was gone.

"Keep pulling," puffed Gertie. "It'll take a while to get him up to the next floor."

What would he find when he got there, I wondered. Another sealed door blocked by a huge cupboard? It must be totally black inside

147

that shaft — like being in a dark closet that was getting smaller and smaller and smaller. What if we squished him against the roof of the shaft? What if … ?

A click from behind us. Then another.

"The door!" hissed Tonchia, sinking her fingernails into my arm. "They are coming downstairs."

Maybe I've moved faster, but I sure can't remember when. I grabbed the panel that had blocked the hole and crammed it back into the opening. No time to move the cabinet back — we'd just have to hope they didn't notice. I pulled Tonchia over beside me so the two of us blocked the panel. Gertie had plopped herself down on a couch and was trying to look relaxed.

"What's going on?" Cecily was down the first three stairs, hunched over and peering around suspiciously. Up in the doorway behind her, I could see Henry's big black shoes. "Who's been making all that racket?"

"It is nothing!" Tonchia's voice was so strong and cheery it surprised me — until I remembered that she was a professional actor. "Just a little game with the children. Why do you bother us?"

"Children?" Cecily glanced around the basement. "Where's that other one? Where's the boy?"

Uh-oh. Silence. A long silence. My stomach tightened as it got even longer …

"He's in the bathroom," said Gertie finally.

Cecily glanced at the door on the other side of the basement, then turned to Henry. "I'll just go down and check."

Check? Oh, please …

But before she could move, Gertie called out in the direction of the bathroom door. "Jesse? They want to make sure you're in the bathroom, dear. Can you just yell out to them?"

What was she *doing?* Jesse was behind *me*, stuck halfway up the wall in a dumb waiter. No way in a million years he could hear her. Even if he could, he'd be yelling from the wrong end of the room.

And then I heard something impossible. Jesse's voice — *from behind the bathroom door!*

"Be out in a minute, Gertie. Sorry I'm taking so long."

If my jaw hadn't been on a hinge, it would have hit the floor.

Cecily grunted and glanced around one more time, her eyes pausing on me. I did my best to look normal — not easy when you're about to keel over from shock. After what seemed like forever, she trotted back up the stairs. The door closed. Gertie let out a wild cackle, then slapped her hand over her mouth and hurried over to Tonchia and me.

"How'd you do that?" I asked.

"Do what?"

"How'd you get Jesse into that bathroom?"

She and Tonchia looked at each other and laughed.

"You mean you don't know?" Tonchia chortled with glee.

"Know what? What are you talking about?"

"Gertie is a ventriloquist!" said Tonchia. "She can throw her voice."

"You mean" — I stared at Gertie — "Jesse's *not* in the bathroom?"

"Of course not. He's up in the dumb waiter, exactly where we left him. I just threw my voice into the bathroom and made it *sound* like Jesse. It's an old trick. I used to do it in variety shows."

"But what — ?" I sputtered. "How — ?"

"Questions later," interrupted Tonchia. "Right now we must help Jesse."

Oh, my gosh! Poor Jesse! Stuck in there alone in the dark, with no idea of what was going on. I pulled the panel off again and stuck my head into the shaft. "Jesse? You okay?"

A single knock came back.

"He wants us to keep pulling."

For the next few minutes, every squeak and moan from the dumb waiter sounded like a thunderclap. I kept waiting for Cecily and Henry to burst through the door again. No way they'd believe that bathroom story twice. Finally, just when I couldn't stand it any more, a hollow knock sounded in the shaft.

We stopped. A second knock.

"He's there." Gertie squeezed my hand and grinned.

I smiled back, but I wasn't quite so sure. Jesse still had to get out through another dumb-waiter door. He still had to get past Cecily and Henry. He still had to get out of the house.

For the next few minutes, we sat, like three mice, listening. I don't know what we expected to hear. If Jesse really escaped, we wouldn't hear a thing. Maybe we were listening for things we didn't *want* to hear. A dumb-waiter door crashing onto the kitchen floor. Jesse's yells as he got captured. Jesse tumbling down the stairs.

Then I heard it. The click and creak of the basement door. I shut my eyes. Cowardly, I know, but I just couldn't stand to see our last plan fail.

Beside me, Gertie breathed a single word. "Jesse."

My heart sank. They had caught him.

"Hurry!" Jesse's whisper. "We've got to be quick."

I opened one eye. He was on the stairs — crouched where Cecily had stood. Behind him, the door yawned open. No Cecily. No Henry.

I couldn't believe it. Jesse Kulniki was actually rescuing us!

He pointed at the open door and put a finger over his lips. Cecily and Henry must be somewhere close by. He beckoned for us to follow. Clutching each other's arms and walking on tiptoe, Gertie, Tonchia and I crept up the stairs. As we got close to the top, I heard voices. Cecily and Henry? No, a TV.

I was the last one up and closed the basement door carefully behind me. Then, edging along in a line, still on tiptoe, Gertie, Tonchia and I followed Jesse down a carpeted hall towards a door. Through a window at the top of the door, I could see starry sky. We were almost out.

Then I saw the other doorway — a wide archway to the room where Jesse and I had first been dragged by Henry. I tried to remember what was in it. A couch, a couple of chairs, lamps, a coffee table and ... a TV. That's where the sound was coming from. But where exactly *was* the TV? Think, Stevie ... Against the far wall, I was sure. If Cecily and Henry were watching it, they'd have their backs to us. We could sneak past them, one at a time.

Jesse obviously had the same idea. When he reached the archway, he stopped and slowly inched his head around. The sound from the TV was louder now — exciting music like you get in an action scene. Henry was saying something, but I couldn't make out the words. Suddenly, Jesse darted past the archway. Yes! He was across. White-faced, tight-lipped, he was practically pasted to the wall on the other side.

Cecily's voice from the living room. A cough.

Next it was Gertie's turn. She peeked around the corner for a long time before she finally made her move. When she did, I nearly chewed my lip off with nervousness. Hurry, I urged her under my breath, hurry. Finally, after what felt like years, she was across, flattened against the wall beside Jesse.

Tonchia next. Oh, man — Tonchia was a poky walker even when she had her cane! She'd never get across without being spotted. Might as well forget it. Might as well just —

Tonchia charged across the doorway. That's right — charged! There she was, beside Jesse and Gertie, waving at me.

Now there was just me left. Piece of cake, right? After all, I *was* the fastest of the bunch. I poked my head around the corner. Cecily sat curled up on a white couch, her back to me. Henry was beside her in a wooden rocking chair, his big feet up on a three-legged stool. Both of them were leaning forward, their eyes on the TV.

Hey! I recognized that movie. It was an old mystery classic that I'd rented. North something. *North by Northwest*, that was it. It was right at the most exciting part. This guy is out on an empty road in the middle of the prairie, waiting for this other guy to show up, and suddenly this little plane comes along and tries to run him down. That's right — a plane! It keeps zooming out of the sky right at him. And the music gets louder and more exciting, and the plane comes down again, and the guy is running, running for a corn field — to hide so the plane won't get him. There he is, he's ducking, he's landing on his stomach, he's —

"Pssssssssssssst!"

Jesse, Gertie and Tonchia were all glaring at me, furious.

Oops!

"Did you hear something?" Cecily's voice from the living room.

Wincing, I jerked backwards. Jesse's eyes were as big as ostrich eggs.

"It's nothing," said Henry. "Just a car outside. On the wet streets."

I took a deep breath. Okay, Stevie, I told myself, that was your last chance to mess up. I counted to three, then shot across that doorway faster than fudge slips down your throat. Good thing, too. Because the moment I was across, I heard Cecily's voice again.

"Wait a minute, Henry."

I stopped breathing.

"What do you mean, wet streets?"

"Shhhh," said Henry. "My favourite bit is coming up."

"But the streets are perfectly dry."

"Shhh — "

"Henry! Listen to me. It hasn't *rained*."

"Move!" I whispered to the others. "NOW!"

CHAPTER

20

THE TV MUSIC BLARED AGAIN — THE SAME exciting music from a moment before. Perfect timing — it covered the sound of the front door opening and four pairs of feet creeping across the porch. My shoulders felt itchy, waiting for a pair of huge, heavy hands to clamp down on them. Jesse started down the porch steps first.

"Watch it!" I hissed.

He froze. The loose stair! Carefully he lifted his foot over it. Turning, he helped Gertie and Tonchia past it, too, while I leaped over. As we crossed the yard, there was still no sound from the house except the TV. Suddenly we were out on the sidewalk! A warm summer breeze ruffled my hair. Above us, a thousand stars winked in the sky.

I searched my memory — wasn't there a convenience store on the corner? It would have a phone for sure.

"This way!" I said.

I did my best to hustle everyone along, but we didn't exactly break any speed records. Tonchia was exhausted. She had to lean on Jesse's arm, and one of her knees was stiff. I moved to her other side and gave her my arm, too.

"Thank you, dear," she murmured. "It's the arthritis."

House by slow house, we hobbled along. I kept waiting for the sickening thud of feet behind us.

Finally it came. Cecily and Henry were through the gate. They were on the sidewalk, down the block — gaining on us with every step. Cecily's arms and legs churned up and down. Henry looked huge — a charging Frankenstein.

"Run!" I yelled. Only two more houses to the store. I could see the sign. Hasty Quick Market.

We ran. Even Tonchia.

Not fast.

But fast enough.

We burst through the Hasty Quick door like an explosion. The clerk, a chubby guy with glasses, clutched at his cash register. A woman pouring herself a coffee splashed some on her hand and squealed. A tall thin man almost shut his arm in the freezer. Even the teenage boys at the video game glanced up.

What was their problem? Hadn't they ever seen a gang of escaped prisoners before?

I looked over my shoulder. There they were! Henry and Cecily were right up to the glass door of the Hasty Quick. Cecily even started to push it open. But Henry pulled her back, shaking his head. I could read his mind. Too many people.

Smart Henry.

"Where's your phone?" demanded Gertie. The

clerk, still stunned, pointed at a pay phone in a corner. Gertie hurried over. Tonchia, Jesse and I watched as Henry and Cecily disappeared into the darkness. Next thing you know, Jesse grabbed my hands, and we were dancing in wild circles, yelling, "We did it! We did it! We did it!" In the background, I could hear Gertie's voice. "Police?"

Jesse and I were laughing and screaming as we flew past the potato chips and chocolate bars. We pounded each other on the back as we whizzed past the breads and buns. I stepped on the freezer man's foot and nearly fell on the bank machine, but that only made us laugh harder. "Free!" we yelled as we whirled past the fax machine.

Whirled past the —

"Jesse! What *time* is it?"

"We're free! We did it! We won! We — "

"JESSE!" I screamed, staring at my watch. "LOOK AT THE TIME!"

He glanced at his own wrist. "It's eleven forty-three."

Charging past the freezer man, I pushed one of the teenagers out of the way to get to the phone.

"They just ran away, officer," Gertie was saying. "Yes, we'll wait here for you. Thanks."

I helped her hang up. Actually, I shoved the receiver back onto the phone hook so hard it clanged. "Where is it?" I blurted.

"Where is what, Stevie? What are you talking about?"

"Your birth certificate! Where is it?"

"My birth certificate? Well, now, just a moment. Let me think."

"No *time* to think, Gertie. Where *is* it?"

Gertie's forehead creased into about fifty little lines. She screwed up her potato nose. "I believe — yes, I'm sure — it's in a book on my bookshelf."

"What book?"

"Now what was it? One of the books my father gave me. *The Count of Monte Cristo?* No. *Great Expectations?* No."

"Gertie, pleeeeeeeeeese."

"Wait now. I think I — yes! *Treasure Island.*"

I grabbed the phone and started to dial. Nothing happened. The dial tone just went on and on.

"Has anybody got a quarter?" I yelled. "Help! Please! A quarter!"

Gertie looked alarmed. So did the clerk, who rushed over to hand me a quarter. I dropped it in the slot. Seconds later, I was talking to my mom.

"Stevie? Is that you? Where are you? What's going on? Where have you — "

"Mom!" I yelled. "Don't say a word. Just listen. It's a matter of — of life and death. Get the master key, Mom, and go into Gertie's apartment. There's a book on her bookshelf — *Treasure Island.* Find it! Then drive as fast as you can to the Hasty Quick Market at Tenth and Harlen. Do you hear, Mom? Fast! We'll be here waiting for you. Thanks, Mom. I love you."

"Stevie, I — "

Hanging up, I sagged against a wall of cookies. Something — a package of chocolate puffs? — bounced off my head. I hardly noticed.

A police car pulled into the parking lot. Gertie

and Tonchia rushed outside and started chattering at three police officers, who took notes and talked on their car phones. The Hasty Quick door opened and a short skinny woman rushed in. She pushed a bill over the counter, grabbed a package of cigarettes and left.

I checked the time. Eleven fifty-three.

A dusty blue car pulled slowly into the lot.

"Mom!" I yelled, charging outside. She and my dad stepped out, and she opened her arms. A hug? Who had time for hugs? There was *Treasure Island,* clutched in her left hand.

"Thanks, Mom." Snatching the book, I raced back into the Hasty Quick.

"A fax!" I hollered, charging up to the counter. "I have to send a fax to London." Riffling through *Treasure Island,* I came upon a loose folded paper. I opened it so fast I almost ripped it in half.

Yes! The birth certificate of Agatha Gertrude Ramsbottom!

I reached into my pocket. Was it still there? Yes! Mr. Throckington-Braithwaite's business card! We had everything we needed now — the birth certificate, the fax number, the fax machine. I couldn't believe it!

I shoved the card and the certificate across the counter at the clerk. "We have to send this right away."

Uh-oh. Why did he look like that? Why was he shrugging? "Uh ... sorry," he said in a hesitant voice. "I think the fax machine is ... uh ... not working."

CHAPTER

21

"WHAT???" I HOWLED. "YOU'VE *GOT* TO BE kidding!"

The clerk's eyebrows wiggled in alarm. I must have looked like I felt — ready to hurl myself onto the tiled floor, kick, scream and burst into sobs.

"Maybe it's just out of paper," he said nervously. "I could give it a try." He stepped out from behind the counter.

"What do you mean — out of paper?" asked the woman with the coffee. "You don't need paper to send a fax. Only to receive one."

"I just started working here — " said the clerk.

"You do so need paper," interrupted the freezer man, reaching for the fax machine. "Here, I'll show you how it works."

"Stevie, will you please explain what's going on here?" My dad blinked in confusion.

"I'm pretty handy with machinery," said one of the video-game teenagers.

The door opened, and a policeman strolled in. Staring down at a pad of paper in his hand, he

160

said, "I need to talk to a — let's see — Stephanie Diamond."

"Nobody explained how to work that machine," apologized the clerk. "How am I supposed to know — "

"Let me take a look at that thing," said the coffee woman, edging between the freezer man and the clerk.

I couldn't take it any more. Throwing my arms in the air, I yelled "WE ONLY HAVE TWO MORE MINUTES!"

I can't even *begin* to describe what happened next. All I can say is that everyone — just everyone — got in the act. The crowd around the fax machine was so thick you could hardly elbow your way in. Somebody was trying to push Gertie's birth certificate into a crack on the machine, somebody else was dialling the fax phone and someone else was pushing buttons. Everybody was talking at once. Everybody had a different piece of advice. Nobody was listening to a single word anybody else said.

It was craaaaaaaaazy!

Suddenly there was a silence.

"It's gone," said the chubby clerk, with a shy smile. "Your fax. We sent it. See? Your paper has come out the other end."

"What time is it?" I asked, not daring to look at my watch. Pleeeeeeeeese, let it be in time ...

The clerk glanced at his wrist. "One minute to twelve."

Some moments are so incredible you can hardly stand to live them. I felt like I was going to burst.

Finally, just this once, and even though I'm not a detective in a movie, I had gotten *something* exactly right. What exploded out of me at 12:00 midnight was a cheer.

"YESSS!!!"

❖ ❖ ❖

The back seat of my parents' car felt as soft and comfy as a feather bed as we drove home. My parents were mumbling in the front, while Jesse and I sprawled, exhausted, in the back. On top of everything else that had happened, we'd spent the past hour telling the whole story — it felt like the fiftieth time — to the police and the people in the convenience store.

Just as we were finishing up, the police got a radio call. Cecily and Henry had been picked up at the airport where they were trying to get on an overnight flight to London. They'd be spending the night in the police station instead.

We might still have been back at the Hasty Quick, except for Tonchia. "You must take me to my home!" she had said to the police officer in charge. "I must sleep. I have tomorrow a very important audition." *Slap!* We'd forgotten all about it. Jesse and I looked at Gertie, who shook her head wearily.

"Couldn't possibly," she said with a little smile. "Tonchia will have to represent all of us."

Tonchia drew herself up to her full height — not quite up to my shoulder, but she seemed a lot bigger. "I will give," she said in a ringing voice, "the performance of my life!" She turned to the nearest police officer. "If you please, young man, a car for me and Mrs. Wiggins."

And now, as I bumped along in the back seat with Jesse, I remembered Tonchia's words. "You gave the performance of *your* life today, Jesse. In that dumb waiter."

"Uh-huh," he mumbled sleepily.

"Weren't you scared? I mean, all those fears of yours — the dark, heights, spiders, closed spaces."

"Terrified."

"So how'd you do it, Jesse?"

"I dunno," he said. "Sometimes you just have to do things. Even if you're scared."

It sounded like something a detective in a movie might say — tough and soft and wise all at the same time. Jesse looked different, too. More grown up, more firm around the chin and eyes. My partner. He grumbles a lot and gets nervous and argues about doing risky things. But right then, I could see what was happening, as clear as a lipstick smear on a glass.

Detecting was giving Jesse Kulniki character.

CHAPTER

22

"A RE YOU, ER, RICH NOW?"

I nudged Jesse under the table. You're not supposed to ask a person straight out if she's rich. Not even if you've helped that person claim an inheritance from her long-lost uncle in England, and you're just dying to know how much she got.

It was two days later, Sunday. Jesse and Gertie and I were sitting in the Versailles Room of the Pacific Grand Hotel at a bright, sunny table in the window. A single red rose stood in a glass vase in the middle, silverware glittered and voices murmured softly. Gertie was treating us to lunch, and we were waiting for Tonchia to join us. Jesse and I were getting our first real chance to talk to Gertie since the Night of the Great Escape. She'd been out all Saturday — first at the police station and then at a lawyer's.

"As a matter of fact," said Gertie with a little-girl kind of grin, "I *am* rich."

"Really?" I said. "You're rich just from Uncle

Cyril's fish-and-chip stand?"

"Well, that was almost fifty years ago." Gertie started buttering a roll from a fancy little plate full of butter flowers. "It seems Uncle Cyril opened a second fish-and-chip shop, then a third and fourth. And then the frozen-food market came along, and what do you think? Uncle Cyril became the biggest producer of frozen french fries in the whole country. Seems that Ramsbottom's Seaside Chips are famous all over England."

"Really?" said Jesse. "With a dumb name like that? Ow, Stevie. Quit kicking me."

"Even the Queen loves Ramsbottom's chips," Gertie went on. "And speaking of fish and chips, I'm getting awfully hungry. Where is that Tonchia? She was supposed to be here ten minutes ago." Gertie peered out the window, checking up and down the street.

"Tonchia has a habit of not showing up on time," I pointed out. "Especially in the Pacific Grand Hotel. As far as I'm concerned, she's four *days* late for lunch."

Jesse was still thinking about money. "How rich *are* you, Gertie? I mean, are you stinking rich? Or just rich-ish? And what are you going to do with your money?"

I'd been wondering, too. What if Gertie bought herself a mansion? What if she moved away?

"Rich enough that I don't have to worry about money," said Gertie. "And rich enough to do some of the things I've been wanting to do."

Like buy a mansion?

"Like start a theatre group." Gertie's eyes

brightened. "I've always loved the theatre. And I have young actor friends who are so talented. But, of course, they haven't got the money to put on the plays they want. So I'm going to become … well, a producer. I'm going to help those young people out."

"Will you be in the plays, too?" I asked.

"Oh, I hope so." Gertie smiled as she took a sip from her water glass. "But only if I'm right for the part. No special treatment."

"Maybe you'll get a chance to do some ventrolo … some vontrilo … some throwing your voice," said Jesse.

Gertie laughed. "Maybe. But I've got other plans, too. I might provide the money for a new little park. My old neighbourhood on the other side of town has got quite run down and could use a spot of grass and some trees. And I could contribute some money to your mother's environmental group, Stevie."

Now that was fantastic news. Garbage Busters, the group my mom works for, is always short of money.

"Other than that, why, I'm quite happy to let life go on more or less as it has."

Good! No mansions. But there was one important thing I had to check out. "Does this mean you're going to be around for the rest of August?"

Gertie must have read my mind. She gave me a wink. "Don't worry — you're both safe. That day camp will have to get along without you."

Jesse squeezed my hand so hard it hurt. We'd done it! We'd beaten Sappy Rabbits!

The waiter crept up behind Gertie with hardly a sound, the same waiter who'd served my other lunch. I sank down in my chair. "Are you ready to order yet, madame?" he murmured to Gertie. I was glad *I* didn't have to talk to him.

"We're waiting for a fourth person," she said. "But what do you say we order some appetizers, kids? Let me see." She ran her finger over the menu. "The *chèvre* sounds good."

"No!"

"Pardon me, Stevie?"

"No goat cheese!"

"Oh," said Gertie uncertainly. "Well, all right. How about the fried chicken wings? Or the fresh pasta?" She nodded at the waiter. "Bring us a tasty assortment. And no, er, goat cheese."

"Very good, madame."

"When will your theatre group start, Gertie?" asked Jesse after the waiter had left.

"We'll begin working on it this fall." Gertie's eyes glittered with excitement. "Oh, the theatre! Being out there in front of a real audience — people clapping, laughing, crying — you can't beat it. I always missed a live audience when I was acting in the movies."

Movies! Something jogged in my brain. That movie magazine on Fantasia's blanket with the blacked-out photograph of Gertie. Quickly, I told Gertie what we'd seen. She shook her head and grunted.

"Foolish snip! She was certainly ticked off at *me*."

"We heard you had a fight in the laundry room. Why was Fantasia so mad?"

The waiter glided up just then with a yummy-looking plate of hot appetizers — chicken bits, deep-fried potato skins, buttery shrimps. We all heaped food onto our plates. Then Gertie said, "Fantasia Bayswater has delusions of grandeur."

Jesse looked at me. I shrugged. "What's that mean?"

"It means she thinks she can become a movie star overnight. Like that!" Gertie snapped her fingers.

"What's that got to do with you?" asked Jesse, picking past a chicken wing to get at the olives.

"She seemed to think I could help her. Wanted me to introduce her to important people in the movies. She expected *me* to get her a starring role." Gertie grunted. "A starring role! Why, the girl's never taken an acting class in her whole life! She thought being pretty was enough. Hmph! Ask Tonchia about that!"

Tonchia?

"What do you mean?" I asked.

"Well, Tonchia and I always figured she'd be swooped up into stardom in Hollywood. She was so beautiful."

Remembering the photographs in Tonchia's apartment, I nodded.

"It didn't happen," Gertie continued. "It was *me* who got the good movie roles. Me — the one who looked like the back of a mud fence. Oh, I was never a big star, but I did okay. More than okay. But poor Tonchia — for all her beauty — only got bit parts. Never did get a decent movie role the whole time we were there."

"Why not?" asked Jesse. "Was she a lousy actor?"

"Not at all. She's a very good actor. And she worked hard. But there are plenty of hard-working, talented actors trying to make it in the movies. For every one who becomes a big star, another thousand never make it. Poor Tonchia was one of the thousand."

"So that's why she's so determined to get the role in *Slap*," I said.

Gertie nodded. "It might be her last chance. But how did we get off on Tonchia? Ah yes, Fantasia. My advice to her was to start at the bottom, and take plenty of acting classes. Acting is a profession, I told her. It takes years of effort to become a decent actor."

"Like learning to play the guitar," said Jesse.

"Exactly. But Fantasia kept saying I could make it easy for her. Said I was just being mean and selfish. Finally, there we were in the laundry room — with her yelling her foolish head off." Gertie made a clucking noise with her tongue.

"So that's why she was reading *Reel West*," I said. "To find a quick way into the movies."

"When she saw Gertie's picture, she must have flipped right out," said Jesse.

I could sort of understand how Fantasia felt. One time I was so mad at my mom I gave her a thick black beard in our family Christmas photo. It took a *lot* of apologizing to get over that one.

"There's something I still don't understand," said Jesse. "Remember that day we walked around Stanley Park, Stevie? Everywhere we went, you kept smelling ripe strawberries. You said it was Fantasia's perfume."

"Oh, uh, yeah." I felt *really* stupid about that

one. "I figured it out, Jesse. It was *you* who smelled like a ripe strawberry."

"Me?" He looked horrified.

"Remember the coat? Your disguise?" He nodded. "Remember I told you I got it at a co-op garage sale? Well, guess who I bought it from."

Jesse's eyes bugged out. "Fantasia?"

I nodded. "Yup. All day long, when I thought I smelled Fantasia, I was really smelling *you* in Fantasia's coat. She must have doused it with a whole bottle of that perfume."

"Oh, my gosh." Jesse's fork clanged onto his plate. "You mean I spent the whole day in … in Fantasia's coat?"

I guess he suddenly realized what he was saying. Fantasia's coat … her strawberry perfume … against his skin … for the whole day. His ears slowly turned scarlet. Then, like paint spilling, the colour seeped across his face and down over his neck.

I guess I could have teased him all the way to bright purple. After all, I now had solid evidence of the most enormous crush in the history of Vancouver. But a person can't control the colour of his ears, can he? I kept my mouth shut.

Maybe I'm getting more sensitive as I get older.

Jesse changed the subject fast — to Howard. "Stevie saw Howard one night wearing *your* gold jacket, Gertie — the one you got from Elvis."

"Mmm, yes, I know. Aren't these crab balls delicious?"

"You *know?*"

"He stole it," she said calmly.

I almost choked on a shrimp. "He what?"

"He came over yesterday to confess," said Gertie. "Poor man was a wreck. When he heard from the Pets Plus woman — Cecily, that is — that I was away on 'holiday,' he started thinking about that jacket. Just couldn't get it out of his mind. Finally he decided that this was his chance to 'borrow' it. Wasn't going to keep it, he said. Just wanted to have it in his apartment for a few days."

"Do you believe him?" asked Jesse. "That he was going to give it back?"

"Oh, sure. Howard isn't really a bad sort, you know. He just wanted the jacket to inspire his music." Gertie laughed. "Can you beat that? Must think you can become a singer by magic."

I remembered the horrible howls coming out of his apartment. If Howard ever became a singer, it would *have* to be by magic.

"How did he get the Elvis jacket?" I asked.

"Easy," said Gertie. "He just knocked on my apartment door one day when Cecily was there. He told her the jacket was his, that he'd left it in my apartment."

"And Cecily gave it to him?"

Gertie nodded. "Just wanted to get rid of him, I guess. Problem was, Howard's basically a decent, honest person. He felt terribly guilty. Couldn't sleep at night trying to figure out how to get the jacket back where it belonged." Gertie sighed. "Poor old Howard. He was so relieved to give it back."

"But how'd he get that sunburn?" I asked. "Jesse and I figured he'd been following us around all day."

Gertie laughed. "Nothing so exciting, I'm afraid. He got that sunburn at the annual picnic of the

Elvis Forever Club. Takes place every year on the anniversary of Elvis's death — August 16. It's the one day Howard stays out in the sun."

Suddenly there was a great flurry of scarves and capes in the doorway. Tonchia was standing there, cheeks flushed. Her smile was so wide it practically leaped off her face.

"Gertie! Jesse! Stevie!" she yelled. "I got it! I got Dr. Kruger!" She swept across the room like a queen.

It was almost as exciting as sending the fax to London. Gertie hugged Tonchia a whole bunch of times, and so did I. Jesse shook her hand so hard she had to tell him to take it easy. Babbling away like that, we caused quite a fuss. I mean, except for our table, this was probably the quietest restaurant in the city.

"Champagne!" Tonchia cried to the waiter, who was looking nervous. "Caviar! Dr. Kruger is mine!" Finally we all settled down, and she explained she was late because she'd been waiting for the movie people to call.

"Finally!" she said for the twentieth time. "A starring role."

"No one deserves it more than you, dear," said Gertie, patting her hand fondly.

We ordered more food, and then Tonchia told us all about the movie. I learned a whole bunch of new movie words. Like *call time* — the time, usually early in the morning, when movie people start work. And *locations* — the places where they film the movies. And *wrap* — when they finish the movie. The most important word, though, was *extra*.

"I am sure I can arrange it," said Tonchia. "They will need children to be extras. Why not Stevie and Jesse?"

"Extra what?" asked Jesse.

"Extras are the people in the background," Gertie explained. "They don't usually say anything. They just walk around in the street or crowd. If it's kids, they might play in a playground."

"I can walk," said Jesse quickly. "I can play. Would we get paid?"

"Of course," said Tonchia. "Everyone in a movie must get paid. But it is not very much money. And it is sometimes very boring. You sit, sit, all day — waiting for your turn in front of the camera."

"That's okay. I'll do it." He thought for a moment. "As long as I don't have to be a mosquito."

Sometimes — I don't know how it happens — my imagination gets carried away. It goes nuts. I'm sorry to say that this was one of those moments.

"Hey, Jesse — we could get discovered! I bet you anything someone will notice how talented we are and … and make up *bigger* parts for us, and — holy moley! We could be in other movies and make tons of money. Maybe we'd even get to be in a TV series and — "

"Stevie!" Gertie shook her head. "Didn't you hear a single thing I said? About Fantasia?"

Fantasia? Oh, gross — did I sound like her?

"Fine," I said, as calmly as I could manage. "We'll be, um, extras. Not much money. Sit around all day, be bored."

I tried to concentrate on Fantasia and Howard — all the trouble they'd gotten into with their

173

daydreams of fame. I really did try.

But I couldn't help it. It was like a giant movie poster had gone up in my brain. It had this huge close-up picture of a girl's face. She had blue eyes, just the right number of freckles and thick, curly brown hair. The hair, I noticed, had been smoothed — probably by the hairdressing people — into long, silky waves. Underneath her face, in gigantic capital letters, it said, STARRING STEVIE DIAMOND.

"Stevie?" Gertie's voice seemed to be coming from a long way off.

Okay, I'd start at the bottom. Acting classes — three a week — no, heck, seven a week. I'd get lots of jobs as an extra, and every time I walked by in the background, I'd smile my most charming smile. The director would just *have* to notice me. It would take a long time — weeks maybe, months —

Maybe it didn't need to take that long. Maybe there was something special I could do in *Slap*. Something I was good at. Something they really needed. Like —

I remembered my scream. *Slap* was a horror movie, wasn't it? They must need somebody who could do a really good blood-curdling scream.

"Stevie?" Gertie sounded nervous. "Is something wrong? You look a little — "

I could feel it building. It filled up my chest like a volcano. It surged up through my lungs and into my throat. No stopping it now. My mouth opened and —

"Stee-veee! Don't!"

I bet you they heard it in Hollywood.

ABOUT THE AUTHOR

When Linda Bailey was a girl she went to a particularly gruesome day camp, a lot like the one that threatens Stevie and Jesse through much of this book. She has never quite recovered. Now she lives in Vancouver, where she spends happier hours at Stanley Park, Locarno Beach and Kitsilano Pool. This is her third Stevie Diamond novel.

Other books in the Stevie Diamond Mystery series:

How Come the Best Clues Are Always in the Garbage?

How Can I Be a Detective if I Have to Baby-sit?

How Can a Frozen Detective Stay Hot on the Trail?

What's a Daring Detective Like Me Doing in the Doghouse?

How Can a Brilliant Detective Shine in the Dark?